"You need a nanny for Rory. I'd like to apply for the job."

Linda didn't know what to say. She would not have been human if she weren't tempted. It would be every woman's fantasy come true to have a man like Nick to come home to every night. But only the very naive would simply accept his proposition at face value.

"Have you returned for a job minding Rory, or to worm your way back into my bed?"

Dear Reader,

A perfect nanny can be tough to find, but once you've found her, you'll love and treasure her forever. She's someone who'll not only look after the kids, but who could also be that loving mom they never knew. Or, sometimes, she's a he and is the daddy they aspire to.

Here at Harlequin Presents, we've put together a compelling new series—NANNY WANTED!—in which some of our most popular authors create nannies whose talents extend way beyond taking care of the children! Each story will excite and delight you and make you wonder how any family could be complete without a nineties nanny.

Remember—Nanny knows best when it comes to falling in love!

The Editors

Look out next month for:

A NANNY IN THE FAMILY
by Catherine Spencer (#1950)

MIRANDA LEE

A Nanny Named Nick

Harlequin Books

TORONTO • NEW YORK • LONDON
AMSTERDAM • PARIS • SYDNEY • HAMBURG
STOCKHOLM • ATHENS • TOKYO • MILAN
MADRID • WARSAW • BUDAPEST • AUCKLAND

ISBN 0-373-11943-7

A NANNY NAMED NICK

First North American Publication 1998.

Copyright © 1997 by Miranda Lee.

All rights reserved. Except for use in any review, the reproduction or utilization of this work in whole or in part in any form by any electronic, mechanical or other means, now known or hereafter invented, including xerography, photocopying and recording, or in any information storage or retrieval system, is forbidden without the written permission of the publisher, Harlequin Enterprises Limited, 225 Duncan Mill Road, Don Mills, Ontario, Canada M3B 3K9.

All characters in this book have no existence outside the imagination of the author and have no relation whatsoever to anyone bearing the same name or names. They are not even distantly inspired by any individual known or unknown to the author, and all incidents are pure invention.

This edition published by arrangement with Harlequin Books S.A.

® and TM are trademarks of the publisher. Trademarks indicated with ® are registered in the United States Patent and Trademark Office, the Canadian Trade Marks Office and in other countries.

Printed in U.S.A.

CHAPTER ONE

FROM the street outside came the low rumble of a motorbike as it burbled into the kerb. Thirty seconds later, the bike's owner appeared in the bar doorway, his tall, broad-shouldered silhouette momentarily blocking out the noonday sun.

Dave glanced up from where he was sitting alone at a table, cradling a schooner of beer. His eyes widened as recognition struck.

Good Lord. Nick! Nick was back from wherever it was he'd disappeared to nearly eighteen months before.

Dave wasn't sure if he was pleased or not. He liked Nick. A lot. He enjoyed his company more than that of any man he'd ever met. But there had been a measure of relief in having his nephew's biological father vanish off the face of the map.

Dave had known right from the start that he should not have allowed Linda to coerce him into finding her a suitable sperm donor for the baby she'd suddenly been determined to have.

But he'd been afraid that if he didn't do what she wanted his headstrong kid sister would simply go off and sleep with someone highly *unsuitable*.

Her long-term live-in lover had just been tragically killed while on a photographic assignment in Cambodia, and Linda had decided to fill the great hole in her heart and her life by having the baby that Gordon had always promised her but never delivered.

Not just *any* old baby, of course. She'd wanted her child to inherit the sort of genes that Gordon would have passed on if he'd lived. Consequently, the sperm donor was to be nothing short of a creative genius. And a perfect physical specimen as well. She'd seen some damned programme on TV about an American clinic which had 'smart' sperm to give to women who wanted good-looking, gifted children and she'd thought the concept quite wonderful!

Naturally, there wasn't such an advanced-thinking clinic in Australia. Neither had Linda's foray to Sydney's sperm bank found even a remote match to her prerequisites for the prospective father of her 'gifted' progeny.

So she'd turned to her big brother—which she only did in moments of dire need—flattering his male ego by saying he must know of *someone* in his circle of smart, sophisticated friends who would fit the bill. Some clever, creative, unconventional fellow who had looks to burn and no qualms about giving some unknown woman the seed of his loins.

Dave had immediately thought of Nick.

Though most wouldn't have.

He smiled wryly to himself as the man in question strode further into the bar, bringing his not inconsiderable physical assets under the overhead lighting.

Tall, dark and handsome was hardly an adequate description. It did fit, superficially. Yet it was far too bland to encompass the complex man Dave had found Nick to be.

When people—and especially women—first looked

at Nick, they never associated him with either intelligence or creativity, except of the most basic kind. Dave could appreciate their mistake. It was difficult to see past that incredible body to the real man inside, or past the highly sexual gleam in those brilliant black eyes to the brains behind them.

Nick was not what he seemed. Aside from his well-disguised IQ he also looked a damned sight younger than his thirty-five years, which meant he could get away with wearing collar-length hair, skin-tight jeans and a black leather jacket with a fierce-looking eagle emblazoned across the back. Dave was barely two years older than Nick, but knew he'd look damned stupid in that get-up.

'Okay if I use the piano, Hal?' Nick asked the barman.

Hal nodded, and those who weren't long-time regulars stared in amazement as this macho-looking bikie walked over to the battered upright piano in the corner, slapped his leather gloves down on the lid, sat down at the scratched wooden stool and began to play a Chopin polonaise.

His long, lean fingers flew over the keys, passionate and note-perfect in their execution. The hotel patrons grew silent as they listened, amazed and intrigued. Classical music might not have been the usual fare offered in this setting but they recognised the brilliance of the player and the contradiction in terms of what they were seeing and hearing.

Nick's fingers flew faster till finally the climax of the piece was reached in one last dramatic, flamboyant flourish of notes. For a few moments, he bent over the keyboard as though exhausted, eyes closed, his unruly black hair falling forward.

But then he straightened, pushed back his hair, closed the piano, stood up and gave a mock bow to his partially stunned audience. Dave began to clap, soon followed by the rest of the Saturday afternoon drinkers.

Nick turned to smile at his friend, then indicated he would get a beer before joining him.

'I see you haven't lost your touch,' Dave complimented Nick when his friend scraped out a chair and sat down.

Nick laughed. 'You've got to be kidding. Rusty as hell, I am. There again, I haven't touched a piano since I was last here.' He lifted the beer to his lips, drinking deeply. 'Ah,' he said appreciatively as he wiped the froth from his top lip. 'That hits the spot. It's damned hot outside for early November.'

'Long time no see, Nick,' Dave said, trying not to sound accusing.

'Sure is,' Nick agreed. 'You're looking well, Dave.'

Dave smiled ruefully at the lie. He'd once been a handsome young man, but life now found him overweight and his light brown hair was thinning. Not that he cared too much; his life didn't revolve around his looks.

'Where've you been?' he asked his friend.

'Around and about.'

Dave shook his head and sighed. 'I see you haven't changed. Just as communicative as ever.'

Nick grinned. 'Come now, Dave, that's not true. You and I have had some of the longest chats in history at this very table. We've discussed everything from A to Z. We've theoretically solved the world's environmental problems, picked every politician alive to pieces and critically analysed just about every book worth reading!'

'That's not what I'm talking about and you know it. Damn it all, Nick, you could have at least had the decency to inform me before you just took off for destination unknown. I thought we were mates.'

'We are. But you know me. Never stay anywhere for long. I get bored.'

Dave wasn't quite sure how long Nick had been a regular here before his disappearance. Only a few weeks, he supposed. It just seemed longer. Nick was a very interesting man to talk to. He'd been to so many places, had seen so many things. He'd done a myriad of jobs as well, from oil-rig worker to short-order cook, from chauffeur to brick-layer. You name it and he'd done it.

'So how long can we expect to have the privilege of your company this time round?'

'God knows. A week. A month. A year. Depends.'

'On what?'

'Hell, Dave, don't ask me. I go with the flow.'

'I'll bet it was a woman,' Dave muttered.

Nick's normally carefree face froze, his dark eyes piercing Dave with a dagger-like glare. 'What in hell are you on about?'

Dave was taken aback. This was a side of Nick he'd never seen before. The sudden switch of mood from easygoing to coldly aggressive was quite startling. Everything about the man had changed in an instant.

His whole demeanour from his body language to his voice, which had dropped to a gravelly growl.

'Nothing to get het up about,' Dave hurried to re-assure him. 'I was just hazarding a guess to the reason for the swift exit from Sydney last time. I thought maybe one of your women might have tried to put the hard word on you for some kind of commitment.'

Nick visibly relaxed, immediately back to being the old familiar Nick again, his very engaging smile car-rying a degree of amusement. 'One of my women, Dave?' He leaned back in the chair and took another deeply satisfying swallow of beer. 'You make it sound like I have a harem.'

'Don't you?'

'Not at all. I'm a one-at-a-time kind of guy.'

'Yeah, right, Nick. One *night* at a time, don't you mean? I've never seen you with the same woman in here two times in a row.'

Nick shrugged. 'Variety is the spice of life, you know.'

'Lucky devil. Still, if I looked like you I'd probably be the same. Though to be honest I think I prefer my own quiet and largely celibate lifestyle. Women are nothing but trouble. So you didn't do a flit because some lovesick dolly-bird was putting the pressure on you for baby bootees and wedding bells?'

'Heavens, no. I never get tangled up with that type of female. Lord preserve me. It *was* a lady, though,' he admitted, 'who brought me *back* to Sydney.'

'Really? I'm all ears. She must be something to bring *you* back for a second serve.'

Nick laughed. 'You wouldn't believe me if I told you.'

'I'd believe anything about you.'

'She's a nun.'

'A nun,' Dave repeated, shaking his head. 'Good God, Nick, aren't there plenty of available women in the world without you hitting on some poor naive creature in a convent?'

Nick laughed. 'Sister Augustine is rising eighty.'

'Oh. In that case, perhaps she's just safe.'

'She practically raised me.'

'No kidding? Do tell.'

'Not much to tell. Her order used to run an orphanage and kids' home in Strathfield. I was dumped on their doorstep one day thirty-five years ago when I was a few weeks old, with a note saying my name was Nick. The nuns, and especially Sister Augustine, brought me up. They gave me the surname of Joseph.'

'Why weren't you adopted out if you were so young?'

'I was supposed to be, but the story goes that every time a couple wanted me, they would take tea with Sister Augustine, after which they would suddenly change their minds and choose another baby. Lord knows what she told them. Maybe that I was mentally deficient, or something equally deflecting. She's always claimed she never said anything detrimental at all. She claims it was God's will that I stayed with them. Anyway, by the time I was around two the nuns stopped showing me to prospective parents and I was safe to be spoilt rotten by them all.'

'See? You had women falling in love with you even back then.'

Nick smiled. It was a soft, sweet smile, giving Dave a glimpse of yet another side to Nick. His sensitive side. 'I think they were just lonely,' he said. 'Especially Sister Augustine. Her maternal instinct was probably starving for someone of her own to mother. Which reminds me, Dave—did I do the trick last year for that couple who couldn't have a child? Is there some bouncing baby boy or cute little girl to gladden that poor woman's unhappy heart?'

Dave was taken aback at Nick's bringing up this subject. After his abrupt disappearance, Dave had never imagined Nick would return, let alone ask about the outcome of his generous act eighteen months before.

Dave wasn't sure what to say. He'd lied to Nick about who it was who'd wanted a sperm donor back then because he hadn't thought Nick would be too wrapped in helping a single woman wanting a baby, let alone Dave's own sister. So Dave had invented an infertile married couple—friends of friends—who were having trouble getting a decent donor from traditional sources.

The temptation to lie again was strong.

Dave pondered his dilemma before rushing into an answer. It didn't seem likely that Nick would ever meet Linda and son. No doubt he'd take off again soon. But, given the slight possibility of an accidental meeting, he could not risk Nick knowing he'd fathered a child somewhere. Nick might take one look at Linda's boy and jump to the right conclusion. Then there would be hell to pay.

'Er...I'm sorry, but no, it didn't take,' he lied again. 'The woman in question was not all that young, you know, so maybe it was all for the best.'

Nick nodded slowly. 'You're probably right. Actually, I did find it a little unnerving later to think I had a child somewhere whom I would never know—and who would never know me in return.'

A mental picture of Linda's incredibly beautiful baby boy popped into Dave's mind. Rory was Nick's offspring through and through: jet-black curls covered his head and his wide dark eyes were bright with intelligence. At nine months old he was already crawling, and even pulling himself up onto furniture. His legs were long and his body strong.

Just like Nick's.

Whilst sentiment whispered to Dave that it was a pity Nick would never know Rory and vice versa, common sense demanded he keep father and son apart. Linda would kill him, for one thing. She'd demanded everyone's identities be kept secret all round. No doubt she wanted to live the fantasy that Rory was Gordon's child.

To be honest, Rory looked nothing like Gordon despite Linda's lover also having been tall, dark and handsome. Gordon had been more of a pretty boy, with an elegant frame. Linda's baby was the spitting image of his real father, whose body was all macho muscle and his facial features chiselled in granite. One look at sire and son together and anyone without preconceived ideas might put two and two together—and get big trouble!

No, Nick could never be told the truth, Dave reaffirmed to himself. There was no reason to feel so guilty about it, either. What Nick didn't know wouldn't hurt him. If Nick had wanted to be a father for real he could have been one by now. He could have married as well.

Dave looked over at his handsome and highly intelligent friend, and wondered why he hadn't. What was it that had set him upon a rolling stone, swinging bachelor lifestyle? Had something happened in his past to turn him off the idea of family and commitment?

Could be, Dave supposed. There were a lot of emotionally damaged people out there these days.

Nevertheless, Nick didn't look at all emotionally damaged as he sat there, sipping a beer, his long legs stretched out before him, ankles crossed. He looked happy with himself, and totally relaxed.

Dave sought a more simple explanation for his friend's rather selfish choice of lifestyle. Maybe that unusual upbringing by nuns hadn't given Nick the example of a normal family life which would make him want it for himself. He'd admitted being spoiled to death. Perhaps he'd grown up never having to satisfy anyone's needs but his own.

Still, that was only speculation.

'Nick?'

Nick took the beer away from his lips and placed it on the table. 'Yep?' he replied equably.

'How come you've never married and had kids?'

Was he wrong or did Nick stiffen again, showing another glimpse of that briefly uptight creature Dave had spotted a while ago?

'Why do you ask?' came Nick's curt enquiry.

'Just curious. You're a good-looking guy. And you're certainly not gay, from what I've observed at first hand. Most straight men get married at some time or other.'

'Marriage is not for me,' he said, again quite curtly.

But then he smiled, and the old Nick was back once more. His black eyes gleamed and his mouth was lightly mocking. 'I could ask the same of you, Dave. Why haven't you a wife and family?'

'I did have a wife. Once.'

Nick just stared at him. He looked quite shocked. 'What happened?'

Dave shrugged. 'Nothing drastic. Just divorce. But it turned me off marriage for life. As for kids... The truth is I can't have any.'

'Oh, God. That's rotten luck, Dave. You'd have been a great father.'

'Well, that's a matter of opinion.'

Actually, Dave was not one of those men who related easily to children. Or babies. He'd made it perfectly clear to Linda from the word go that she wasn't to expect him to babysit except in cases of extreme emergency. He'd told her quite firmly that if she was silly enough to become a single mother on purpose, then the responsibility was hers and hers alone.

Linda had scoffed at ever needing her brother's non-existent babysitting abilities. The dear girl had gone into unmarried motherhood with rose-coloured glasses, only to discover it wasn't nearly as easy as she'd thought it would be.

Postnatal depression and an inability to breastfeed had been dismaying starters, gradually followed by the grim acceptance that good parenting was not something that miraculously happened on the birth of one's baby, however wanted and loved that baby might be. There were some women who, while they loved their offspring to death, just weren't cut out to be with them twenty-four hours a day, seven days a week.

This realisation had depressed Linda all the more.

But, Linda being Linda, she hadn't wallowed in her own weaknesses for too long. She'd hired her widowed neighbour to be Rory's minder during the day and had gone back to work. She wasn't totally happy with the situation, but she was at least sane.

Linda's experience confirmed to Dave that the Sawyer siblings were not natural parents, and that being childless was not the end of the world.

'To be perfectly frank,' he told Nick now, 'I'm not unhappy with the status quo. I've always been married to my job. And children have never been a priority with me, even before I knew I was sterile. My wife was right to divorce me. She now has a new husband and three incredibly noisy boys.'

'So how is the job down at the paper?' Nick asked.

'Flat out as usual. I came here straight from the office. Worked all night and all morning getting Sunday's edition ready. I'm just about to go home to bed and I don't intend resurfacing for the next twenty hours. But first I think I'd better visit the Gents. That beer's gone straight through me. Mind my mobile, will you? When you're a journo they never leave you alone for too long. If it rings, answer it and tell whoever it is that I'm in a coma.'

CHAPTER TWO

NICK watched his friend make his way tiredly across the floor. Poor Dave. He felt sorry for him. He had nothing in life but that pathetic newspaper he worked on. Still, he could well understand that Dave might not want to marry again after his first marriage had ended in divorce. One bitten, twice shy was something Nick could relate to.

He frowned darkly for a moment, then shuddered. Don't start thinking about that, man, he ordered himself.

His mind swung to the news Dave had given him about his failure to father a child for that unhappy, unfulfilled woman. He wasn't sure if he was disappointed or relieved.

Initially, the thought that he'd given some unknown woman the baby she so desperately wanted had made him feel good. But then his feelings on the matter had changed. The idea of being a father had begun to both disturb and absorb him.

Within a week of handing his specimen over, Nick had felt the urge to find out who this woman was, and what she looked like, whether she would make a good mother and whether he'd done the right thing in giving her the wherewithal to have his child.

His child. Not her husband's.

That was why he'd fled Sydney eighteen months before. Because he'd known if he stayed, he might put such a search into reality. Yet he'd known that to do so would be very wrong.

So he'd taken off around Australia again, seeking distraction from his disturbingly compulsive feelings. But nothing had totally emptied his mind of thoughts of his unknown offspring, and in the end he'd been forced to return and confront what was eating away at him—only to find out that the mystery child which had haunted his head did not exist! Had never, ever existed!

Again he felt a fierce jab of disappointment.

Male ego, Nick supposed ruefully. That perverse part of the male psyche which drove one to do stupid things and feel stupid things. He should be grateful that he'd failed to impregnate that woman. He didn't want to bring a child into this world, even an unknown one. What was the matter with him? He'd given up being a masochist ten years ago, and he didn't aim to start again now!

He was scowling down into his beer when the beep of Dave's mobile phone made him jump. A quick glance across the room showed no sign of Dave's return, so he picked up the phone and pressed the answer button.

'Dave's phone,' he said.

'I must speak to Dave,' a female voice said impatiently. 'Is he there? This is Linda. His sister.'

Nick blinked his surprise. He'd had no idea Dave even *had* a sister. There again, neither of them had spoken to each other on any personal level before today. Their previous Saturday afternoon drinking discussions had always been typically male—competitive, argumentative, analytical. And totally impersonal and objective.

'He can't come to the phone at the moment,' Nick told Dave's sister. 'Can I take a message?'

'Who the hell are you?' she demanded to know. She sounded irritable.

'My name's Nick. I'm a friend of Dave's.'

'Where *is* Dave, damn him? He's always complaining that he has to keep that phone glued to his side, but the one time I need to talk to him he's not there!'

'He's in the Gents. We're at the pub. Can I help?'

'At the pub,' she said tartly. 'Would we all be that lucky! At least he won't be able to tell me he can't help me out this afternoon if all he's got to do is drink himself silly.'

'Help you out with what?' Nick asked.

'My front lawn, that's what.'

'What about your front lawn?'

'My mower-man didn't come today. I just rang him and he's come down with some bug or other, but I simply have to have that lawn mowed today. I'm having people over tonight, and after all the rain we've had this past fortnight the grass is up to my knees. So where *is* that brother of mine? Surely he's out of the Gents by now.

'Yes, Sue, I won't be much longer!' she yelled to someone in the background.

'I hate to tell you this, Linda, but I don't think Dave's in a fit state to mow lawns today. He's absolutely exhausted after working all day and night at the paper.'

'Oh, for pity's sake, you don't think I'll fall for

that rubbish, do you? Put Dave on, please,' she insisted snippily.

'I told you, he's in the Gents. And then he's going home. To bed. Look, give me your address and I'll pop over and mow the lawn for you.'

'What?'

'You heard me.'

'And why, pray tell, would you do that? You don't even know me!'

Yep. She was definitely irritable.

'I'm Dave's best mate.' A little exaggeration never hurt, Nick thought. Besides, he was rather enjoying sounding noble in the face of the prickly Linda's lack of compassion. 'Mates help each other out in times of need.'

'Oh.' She sounded mollified. Or perhaps ashamed of herself for her stroppy attitude. 'All right, then. I won't look a gift-horse in the mouth. Thanks,' she added grudgingly, and gave him an address in Balmain, which was blessedly no more than twenty minutes away from the inner-city hotel he was sitting in at that moment. 'The equipment's in the garage,' he was informed brusquely. 'Just knock and Madge will show you where. I'll call her and tell her you're coming.'

'You're not at home?'

'No, I'm at work, worse luck.'

Nick wondered who Madge was. Friend? Flatmate? Another sister?

'Okay. Don't you worry, Linda. Your lawn will be done this afternoon. You have my word.'

'That's very sweet of you. Nick, is it?'

'Yep. That's my name.'

She sighed, and the sound immediately made Nick think of sex. He'd always been partial to women who sighed a lot when he made love to them. Especially afterwards.

'Look, I'm sorry if I was rude just now,' she apologised, another sigh doing nothing to lesson the image he suddenly had of her lying back naked in his bed. 'Life has been damned difficult lately, what with one thing and another. Yes, Sue, I said I was nearly finished! Sorry. An anxious female panting on a call from the boyfriend. Still, I must go. Deadlines.' And she hung up.

Deadlines? Nick raised his eyebrows. Another journalist in the family, no doubt. He wondered what Dave's sister looked like, and if she was single. She'd sounded younger than Dave, and not particularly married. A married woman would have had a husband to do her lawns. Unless she was divorced, of course. Women who worked on weekends often found themselves divorced. Being a dedicated career woman was not conducive to harmony in the marital home.

Nick was partial to dedicated career women. They liked their sex without the complications of love and commitment, which was the only way Nick would have it these days.

'Who was that on the phone?' Dave asked wearily as he settled back in his chair. 'Not the paper, I hope?'

'Nope. Your sister. I didn't know you had a sister, Dave. You never mentioned her.'

Dave seemed struck speechless for a moment. But then he laughed. 'You don't honestly think I'd tell *you* about any sister of mine, do you?'

'Ah, she's a looker, is she? I imagined as much.

You're a fine-looking fellow, and good genes usually run in the family. How old is she, by the way?'

'None of your damned business. So what did she want?'

Nick could see Dave wasn't too pleased about his having any personal contact with his sister—and who could blame him? So he decided that a little lie of omission was called for.

'She was going to ask you to mow her lawn this afternoon. Her usual mower-man is sick.'

'And?'

'I told her you were much too tired from working all night at the paper, that you were about to go home to bed and she was to get someone else. She said she would, and hung up.'

Dave seemed amazed. 'Really? Just like that? Linda hung up just like that?'

Clearly this was not usual Linda behaviour. Nick decided, in the interests of credibility, to elaborate somewhat.

'Well, she wasn't too thrilled at first, but I was very forceful in convincing her of your exhausted state. In the end, she quite happily agreed to follow my suggestion.'

'You're a true friend, Nick.'

'You'd better believe it. Now, off home to the kip for you, I think. I'll see you here next Saturday, if not before.'

'You're a good bloke, Nick. I didn't mean to offend you about Linda. It's just that…well…'

'She's your little sister and you want the very best for her,' Nick finished wryly.

'Something like that.'

'So how old *is* this sweet young thing you're so keen to protect?' he asked, even more curious now.

Nick found Dave's hesitation to answer really quite odd. Linda hadn't sounded at all like the sort of woman who needed an older brother for a keeper.

'Thirty-one,' he said at last.

'Hardly a child, Dave,' Nick reminded him. 'Besides, she sounded like she could handle herself very well.'

Dave chuckled. 'She can be a tough little cookie when she's riled. I'll give her that.'

'So stop worrying about her,' Nick advised. 'She won't thank you for it, if I know women.'

'You don't know Linda,' Dave said drily.

'Wild, is she?'

'No, not wild. Just bloody-minded at times.'

Nick could believe that. Beautiful women were often strong-willed. And Linda Sawyer was bound to be beautiful. Her brother would not worry so much about her if she wasn't.

It was a pity, Nick decided, that she was at work today. He would have liked to see this Linda in the flesh.

His own flesh suddenly stirred, surprising him—till he recalled it had been some time since he'd been to bed with a woman.

He wasn't quite the indiscriminate womaniser Dave believed him to be. Sex was, however, very important to him. He did not like to go too long without the pleasure—and tranquillising effects—of a woman's body. Regular lovemaking soothed the demons which dozed—not deep enough—within his soul.

'Go home, Dave,' he advised, his voice a little

sharp. Frustration did not sit well on Nick. It made him edgy.

Dave didn't seem to notice anything. He nodded, slipped his mobile into his pocket, then left.

Nick's dark gaze swept the room, noting a woman sitting alone over in a corner, sipping a drink and dragging on a cigarette. When his eyes met hers she stared back boldly, invitingly. She was good-looking enough from a distance. But cheap. Nick was never attracted to cheap. Which was a pity. Cheap was far easier to meet and pick up than classy.

Irritated, he stood up abruptly, stalked over to snatch up his leather gloves from the piano then whirled to stride towards the door.

The sun outside was even warmer than when he'd arrived. Summer was still three weeks away, but the heat and the humidity were oppressive.

Mowing a lawn in this heat would do him good, Nick decided as he straddled his Harley-Davidson and pulled on his gloves. Hard physical labour invariably made him forget about sex. That was why he often worked at physical jobs. Still, he hoped it was a large lawn. A *very* large lawn!

CHAPTER THREE

IT WAS minute. Two small rectangles of ankle-length grass on either side of a central path. There weren't any garden beds or bushes, and most of the narrow front yard was taken up with the even wider cement driveway which dipped down to the double garages jammed hard against the left boundary of the block.

The house itself, however, was not at all minute. It was two-storeyed, its flat cement-rendered façade covering the rest of the block from the garages to the right boundary. Brown and white striped awnings broke the expanse of stark white walls, and shaded the west-facing windows. Terracotta tiles covered the pitched roof.

One only had to glance at all the other dark brick nineteen-twenties federation-style houses which lined the street to know that this particular residence was a recent and very modern renovation and addition.

Nick could not believe for a moment that Dave's sister owned this place. A new house this size in Balmain, down near the water, would cost the earth! Journalists, unless of the famous television variety, did not earn enormous salaries.

Which turned his mind to the mysterious Madge. Was she a wealthy girlfriend with whom Linda lived? One of those sleekly groomed and glamorous women who believed you could never be too rich or too thin?

Nick pressed the bell on the super-stylish recessed

door and waited for Madge to show her wares. He kept a superbly straight face when a very plump elderly lady answered the door. She had short grey permed hair and was puffing with exertion, probably from hurrying down the steep staircase Nick could see behind her.

When she looked him up and down with a hint of old-fashioned disapproval in her narrowed eyes, Nick was glad he'd left his leather jacket and gloves stuffed in his rucksack on the back of his bike. He didn't think he looked too disreputable in jeans and a white T-shirt, though nothing could hide his unshaven state—which seemed to be capturing Madge's critical attention.

Nick was glad the Harley was out of sight as well. He'd left it on the other side of the high, cement-rendered wall which enclosed the block and hid the offending lawn from the street.

'Nick, is it?' she speculated at last.

'That's me.' He smiled, having slotted her happily into the role of maiden aunt or pensioner boarder. Much better than lesbian lover. 'And you must be Madge!'

His easy smile seemed to do the trick. She smiled back, all her earlier wariness disappearing.

'Yes, it is. My, but it's hot out here, isn't it?'

'Sure is.'

'Come inside. Would you like a cool drink before you start on the lawn? Or should I lead you straight through to the garage and the mower?'

'I think I'd better mow first and drink afterwards. I wouldn't be surprised if it storms later.'

She peered past his shoulder up at the clear blue

sky. 'Really? Oh, I hope not. Linda will be so disappointed if it rains. She wants to serve dinner out on the back terrace tonight.'

Maybe Madge is a cook, Nick reassessed.

'Come through this way,' she said, and bustled off to her right.

Nick followed, closing the front door against the hot afternoon sun and quickly heading in Madge's wide wake. The downstairs interior was pleasantly cool and had one of those open-plan designs, with polished parquet floors, high ceilings and no doors, only tall, wide archways.

Nick glanced around as they moved into a huge rectangular living room which was divided into two distinct areas by three wide wooden steps. In the middle of the closest area, sitting on a multicoloured Persian rug, was a very expensive-looking black leather sofa with matching lounge chairs grouped around a glass-topped coffee table.

Down the dividing steps, in the slightly smaller sunken area, rested a matching glass-topped dining table surrounded by six black leather chairs. A huge black stone figurine of a panther crouched in the centre of the table top. Even from a distance the big cat looked both original and priceless.

Other than that one piece, however, there were no other *objets d'art* in the sparsely furnished area. No sculptures in the bare corners. No paintings on the stark white walls, which were only broken by a fireplace framed in black ironwork.

Still, Nick liked the stark simplicity of the decor. He'd never been one for clutter.

'Nice place,' he murmured.

'Linda hasn't finished decorating the downstairs yet. But it's going to be lovely.'

Nick absorbed this information with a degree of surprise, for it certainly sounded as if Dave's sister *did* own this house. You didn't go to so much trouble decorating a rented establishment. Had she won the lottery? Or been a workaholic since the year dot and saved all her pennies?

Perhaps she and Dave had inherited money, Nick speculated. He knew next to nothing of his friend's finances. Just because Dave frequented a very ordinary hotel, that didn't mean he and his sister weren't wealthy.

But money could never buy style, and that was what this place had—style. Nick hoped that 'finishing decorating' didn't mean putting curtains up at the far wall, which was ninety per cent glass and gave a spectacular view of the highly original back yard and the harbour beyond.

The block sloped very steeply at the back, the land covered by a series of flagged terraces. On the top level sat an eclectic but attractive selection of outdoor furniture flanked by huge pots full of flowering plants. Nick could imagine that sitting out there on a balmy spring evening would be very pleasant, provided it didn't rain. But the dark clouds already gathering on the horizon did not herald well for Linda's outdoor dinner-party plans.

'This way,' Madge said, opening a white door which had been well camouflaged in the white wall. It led down several steps into the double garage, which housed more crates and cardboard boxes than Nick had ever seen. No car, but there was room for one. Just. Either Linda didn't have one or she'd driven it to work.

'The mower's in the corner over there,' Madge pointed out. 'Try not to be *too* noisy—I've just got the baby to sleep.'

Nick looked up, startled. 'Baby? What baby?'

'Linda's, of course.' Madge frowned at him, while Nick tried not to look too taken aback. 'I thought you were a friend of the family?'

'Not really. I'm Dave's friend. Linda and I have never met.'

'Oh, *Dave*.' Madge pulled a face. 'He's been absolutely useless, that man. He acts like he's scared stiff of Rory, but I think it's all just a ploy to get out of babysitting.'

Nick deduced that Rory was the baby.

'And the baby's father?' Nick asked, intrigued. No wonder Dave was worried about his sister. Being an unmarried mother was not uncommon these days, but it was still not an ideal situation.

Madge tut-tutted. 'Now that's a sad story. The baby's father was killed—blown up by a land-mine in Cambodia. Linda was with him at the time. She's a journalist, you know, and he was a very famous photographer. They went everywhere together. They simply lived for each other.'

Madge suddenly became a little teary. 'Poor thing. She didn't even know she was pregnant when the accident happened. Not only that, they'd been finally going to get married when they came home.'

Nick's heart contracted. What a bloody rotten world it was. He shook his head sadly. 'What terrible luck.'

'Yes. I don't know how Linda's coped, I really don't. But she's a very brave lady. We've been neighbours for ages, you know, but, strangely, I didn't get to know her till some time after Gordon was killed. They bought the original house together some years back, then had it done up. Actually, they were as good as married. I used to think they were. Of course, they weren't here all that much. Always flitting around the world on some assignment or other, those two. He'd take the photographs and she'd write the stories.'

Nick didn't say a word for fear of stopping the woman's flow of gossip.

'Anyway, one day late in her pregnancy Linda appeared on my doorstep and asked if she might come in for a cup of tea and a chat. She was so lonely, the poor love. As I said, that brother of hers is useless. And her parents have passed on, so she has no mother to turn to.

'After that she used to visit me nearly every day and we became firm friends. When Rory was born and she had so much trouble with him it was me she turned to for advice. Quite desperate she would get some days. I did all I could to help her, but, quite frankly, Linda's just not one of those girls who took to motherhood and staying at home all the time. It drove her crazy.'

'It can't be easy with no father to help,' Nick murmured sympathetically.

'Yes, you're quite right. Still, with a bit of luck Linda will find someone else to marry her eventually, and to be a father to Rory. She's a good-looking girl. Meanwhile, I was only too happy to come in and mind Rory when she went back to work,' Madge raved on.

'Though he's a bit of a devil at times. High-spirited, like his mother. Oh, goodness, listen to me, gossiping away and probably boring you to death. I'd better check on Rory, and you'd better get on with mowing that lawn!'

Nick did just that, but his mind remained with Linda's story. It was really tragic, he thought. Dave's sister didn't sound as if she was coping all that well. But he didn't think the answer was for her to race out and marry again. He'd seen some disasters with unsuitable stepfathers who didn't have it in them to love and care for another man's child.

Still, it wasn't any of his business, was it? He was only here to mow the lawn.

It only took him fifteen minutes to complete the job. When he stopped the mower and wheeled it back into the garage, the muffled sound of a baby crying filtered through the door which led back inside the house.

Nick sighed his regret at waking the child, but there was nothing he could have done about it. Mowing lawns was a noisy occupation. It was also a hot one. Even in that short space of time, beads of perspiration had pooled all over his upper body, and the T-shirt was clinging to his back. He decided to take up Madge's offer of a cool drink before he got back on his bike and headed home to the convent.

The baby's crying seemed to grow louder and more frantic in the minute it took Nick to return the mower to its place in the corner of the garage then pull down the rolling door. When he opened the door which led into the interior of the house, his ears were blasted with high-pitched cries which alternated between shrieks and sobs.

Why in God's name didn't Madge go and see to the child?

Nick frowned as he strode across the living-room floor. He did not approve of the idea of letting a baby cry itself back to sleep—not when that crying had gone beyond crying to hysteria.

The unexpected sight of a very still Madge lying at the bottom of the stairs was self-explanatory. Nick sucked in a shocked breath then raced to see to the inert figure's plight.

A pulse reassured him she was still alive. Her colour wasn't good, however. He wondered if she'd had a fall or a coronary. He was about to start resuscitation procedures when Madge groaned, her eyelids fluttering open.

'What happened?' Nick asked swiftly.

Her eyes closed for a moment, then opened painfully again.

'Fell,' she rasped. 'Dizzy. My side hurts. I think I might have broken something.'

'I'll call an ambulance straight away,' he said, glancing around. 'Where's the phone? Right, I see it. Hang on, Madge. We'll have you in hospital before you can say lickety split.'

'Rory,' she croaked weakly as the baby's cries heightened even further, if that were possible.

'Is he in a cot?'

'Uh-huh.'

'Then he'll live. You come first, Madge. After I've rung the ambulance I'll go get him.'

'All right,' she agreed, sighing.

Nick dialled the emergency number and was assured an ambulance would be dispatched immediately. Then he dashed up the stairs, following the racket to a bedroom where a red-faced infant of perhaps twelve months was standing in his cot, screaming and shaking the sides as though the hounds of hell were after him. Nick took one look at the fury of the child's tantrum, at his big liquid dark eyes and thick mop of black curls, and decided his father must have been in the Mafia.

On sighting Nick, Rory stopped mid-scream for a split second, as though assessing this stranger who didn't look at all like his mother or Madge. And then he found his second wind and began to bawl again, even more fortissimo than before.

Nick shrugged, walked over and scooped him up, balancing him on his hip and ignoring his piercing protests.

'Do shut up, Rory,' he said sternly. 'Madge is hurt and the last thing she needs is to listen to your infernal wailing.'

Rory fell silent a second time, round eyes inspecting this person who knew his name and who spoke with such authority. Nick noticed there wasn't a real tear in sight on his chubby cheeks.

He smiled wryly. 'You old faker, you.'

Rory suddenly smiled back, a gloriously brilliant smile which showed the beginnings of a tooth just breaking through his gummy mouth.

Nick felt something curl around his heart, then squeeze tight. The sensation shocked then annoyed him.

'Not on your life, you little con man,' he muttered

as he carried the child from the room. 'You can't get round me as easily as that.'

But it seemed he could.

As could Madge.

Nick found himself promising her all sorts of things—the main one being that he would stay and look after Rory till his mother got home.

'If you think you can manage, that is,' Madge added faintly.

Unfortunately, Nick had already shown how well he could manage during the fifteen minutes it took the ambulance to arrive. In that short space of time he'd made Madge comfortable on the floor, changed Rory's nappy and given him some orange juice. The child had really taken to him, too. Either that or he liked playing with his hair, which, though not really long, was a darned sight longer than Madge's tight frizzy curls.

Whatever, there was not a peep of further protest from his rosebud mouth, which was apparently unusual. Rory, Nick was beginning to appreciate, had a reputation not dissimilar to Linda's—he could be...difficult.

Unfortunately, however, his mother could not be contacted before Madge's departure. Her work number was engaged. So Nick's promise to stay with Rory till his mother got home looked like being more than a simple half-hour of emergency babysitting. Madge said Linda should be home by five at the latest, but that was a couple of hours away.

Still, what else could he do? Madge was in pain and had enough to worry about. Luckily, he'd been able to contact Madge's eldest daughter, who lived on the North Shore and said she'd go straight to the hospital.

After the ambulance left, Nick carried Rory outside where with one hand he wheeled his much valued bike inside the walled-in front yard. He didn't mind playing knight to the rescue, as long as he didn't lose his trusty steed. Tossing his equally trusty rucksack over his spare shoulder, he went back inside and set about filling in the time till Rory's mother came home.

He found a television in a family room upstairs, and sat watching a football match with Rory on his lap. By half-time Rory was beginning to droop, so Nick put him back in his cot and was gratified when those big dark eyes closed.

He watched the sleeping child for a while, fascinated by the way his baby lips made little in-and-out movements as he slept. He wasn't twelve months old, as he'd first thought. He was just on nine months, Madge had informed him.

'Cute little beggar,' he said as he turned and tiptoed from the room.

Nick tried Linda's number again. Still engaged. Frustrated, he rang Sister Augustine and explained he might not arrive tonight after all, giving him plenty of leeway. He didn't explain what he was doing, for fear of all the wrong conclusions she might come to. Sister Augustine had for too long tried to talk him into settling down, and Nick did not want to give her false hopes. He just told her he'd been held up on the road with mechanical difficulties.

After he hung up, he tried Linda's work number again. Still engaged. He bet it was an office full of women. Women sure liked to talk. Sister Augustine would rattle on for hours whenever he visited, questioning and probing, wanting to hear about everything he'd done since his last visit. But she wasn't content with finding out the whats and wheres; she always wanted to know the whys and the wherefores.

And she always asked him how he was *feeling* these days. Didn't females know a man liked to keep his feelings to himself? Why did they always have to chip away at you till you either exploded or simply walked away?

Nick was scowling as he marched back upstairs to check on Rory. But his scowl softened to a smile when he peeped over the side of the cot. Sleeping like a baby. All that yelling must have tired him out.

Nick's watch showed three-twenty—still ages away from Linda's anticipated home time. He rubbed the stubble on his chin. A shave was called for, he decided. And a shower. He couldn't have the lady of the house thinking he was some kind of yobo.

But first he did a swift reconnoitre of the top floor. There was a bathroom right next to Rory's room, separating the nursery from a large bedroom which opened out onto a back balcony with an even better view of the harbour than downstairs. On the other side opposite the nursery lay a third, smaller bedroom plus the family room where Nick had already spent some time and which also led out onto that same back balcony.

The decor upstairs was cosy and comfy as opposed to the starkly modern look of downstairs. Wall-to-wall smoky grey carpet covered all the floors. The spacious family room was especially relaxing, and very functional.

A huge wrap-around sofa covered in royal blue velvet faced the large entertainment unit which contained a television, video and sound system. There was a large grey granite-topped bar in one corner which doubled as a kitchenette. Besides the small built-in fridge, there was a long counter against the wall behind, carrying all sorts of cooking equipment from a microwave to a kettle and a toaster. Spacious under-counter cupboards carried a supply of drinks, glasses, crockery, cutlery, coffee, tea, biscuits and baby foods.

Nick assumed there was another, larger kitchen downstairs—he hadn't looked around down there properly yet. But for now this one sufficed his and Rory's needs. If Linda didn't come home by dinner time he might have to go down and see what other food supplies were in stock. But he figured she would be home long before then since she was planning a dinner party tonight.

Another glance at his watch showed three-thirty. Time for that shower, he thought, and headed for the bathroom.

Nick had a tendency to sing in the shower. Opera, mostly. Or one of those old Mario Lanza numbers the good sisters had fed him on during his growing-up years. Especially the religious ones.

He had a good tenor voice too, and launched into one of his favourites while he soaped and shampooed. He entirely forgot about Rory, and was still in full voice when he snapped off the water and heard the baby's cries.

The next line of his song was immediately replaced

by an expletive which would have made both Sister Augustine and Mario Lanza blush. Nick swiftly wrung out his dripping hair, wrapped a navy blue bath sheet around his hips and strode from the steam-filled room.

'Keep your nappy on!' he called out as he reached for the doorknob to Rory's room. Once again, Rory shut up the second Nick appeared in the doorway.

Nick halted, his big hands finding his hips. His mock glare was accompanied by glittering black eyes. 'I have a feeling you need some discipline, young man. I've a good mind to leave you there while I go and get dressed.'

When Rory gave him one of those glorious grins of his, Nick relented. 'You're worse than even the most beautiful woman,' he said, shaking his head as he came forward to scoop the child up again. 'I just can't say no to you. Come on; you can watch me make myself respectable for your mother.'

Once settled on Nick's hip, Rory immediately picked up a wet lock of Nick's hair and stuffed it in his mouth, sucking on it as if he were dying of thirst.

'Oh, so it's a drink you'd be wantin', is it?' Nick teased in an Irish accent as he made his way from the room. 'It wasn't more of me fine singin'?'

He came through the doorway and was about to turn right to go down to the family room when something at the top of the stairs caught his eye.

His head jerked round to encounter a woman with eyes like steel daggers bearing down on him with a very heavy-looking brass lamp base in both her hands, raised up over her right shoulder like a fairway wood about to claim a divot or two. In Nick's head.

'Hey!' Nick shouted, and jumped back out of her way.

She stopped bearing down, but not the glaring. And that lamp remained threateningly raised. 'You'd better have a damned good explanation of what you're doing with my baby,' she warned in gravelly tones. 'Or you're dead meat, mister!'

Nick almost smiled. The mother tigress was coming to the defence of her cub, regardless of the odds. Didn't she know she wouldn't have stood a chance against him if he really had been a bad man intent on murder and mayhem? He was six feet four inches tall, weighed over one hundred kilos and had black belts in karate and judo. She looked about five-four and could weigh no more than fifty kilos.

But, of course, she didn't know that, he realised wryly. Neither did she care. She would fight to the death for her child.

Nick warmed to her immediately. No surprise, really. He'd known from the first moment he'd spoken to her on the phone that he'd like Dave's spirited sister.

'I'm waiting,' she snarled.

Nick suppressed another smile of admiration. 'I'm Nick,' he said. 'You know. Dave's friend who came to mow your lawn?'

Her fierce expression didn't relax for a second. 'In that case, what are you doing inside, half-naked and holding my baby?' she demanded to know. 'And where the hell is Madge?'

'Madge fell down the stairs. She might have broken her hip. She's in hospital.'

'Oh, no!' Her fierce face finally fell. The lamp base

was lowered and she just stood there, looking shattered. Her head drooped, and she began shaking it from side to side.

It gave Nick the opportunity to look her over without appearing to be rudely staring.

She would be a really striking woman if she ever took some trouble with her appearance. As it was, she was wearing no make-up and her honey-brown hair was scraped back from her face and twisted into a knot so tight that not a single hair would dare to escape. But nothing could disguise the fine features in her face.

Her figure was another matter. Although obviously slim, it was impossible to gauge her shape, hidden as it was in severely tailored navy trousers, a plain white shirt and an oversized navy linen jacket.

If she'd been trying for a feminist look, then she'd almost succeeded. Nick itched to take her hair down and get those hideous trousers off her.

Suddenly, her quite lovely blue eyes snapped up to glower at him once more. 'And just when did this all happen?' she demanded to know.

Nick shrugged. Rory had stopped sucking his hair and was looking at his mother, but he was making no indication that he wanted to go to her. He seemed very happy where he was.

'A little over an hour ago. After I'd finished doing the lawn, Rory here was crying his head off. When he didn't stop, I came inside to check and found Madge at the bottom of the stairs. She'd fainted after her fall. But she came round.'

'Why didn't you call me at the office?' Linda continued accusingly. 'Madge knows my number.'

'I tried. It was engaged. In fact, I've tried on and off ever since but it's always engaged.'

'Sue!' Linda spat, practically stamping her foot at the same time. 'She thinks that phone's her own personal social line. I'll have something to say to her when I get in to work on Monday.'

She glared at him again with furious blue eyes. Nick wasn't sure if they were for him or the hapless Sue. 'That doesn't explain why you've got no clothes on,' she persisted, all the while looking him up and down with decided disapproval.

Nick was beginning to feel a tad irritated, despite understanding her reaction. 'I was taking a shower,' he explained in level tones. 'And I *was* going to shave.'

She stared at the two-day growth on his chin, then at his hair, which, uncombed and wet, probably looked as wild as the rest of him.

'Is that your motorbike in the front yard?' she quizzed.

'Yeah. Why?'

'And you're a friend of *Dave's?*' she asked sceptically.

He could see the way her mind was working, and didn't like it one bit. His earlier admiration for her took a nosedive. Nothing turned Nick off a woman quicker than her looking down her nose at him.

'Why shouldn't I be?' he countered icily. 'You got something against blokes who ride bikes? Yeah, I see you have. Pity. Don't worry, honey, it's not contagious. Here. Take your kid. Thank God he's still at that age where his parent's prejudices don't affect his judgement.'

Nick took an angry step towards her, holding Rory out at arm's length. Rory immediately started to cry. His mother reached to take him when something happened which stopped the two grown-ups in midstream.

The navy towel which had been roughly slung around Nick's hips slipped its moorings and slithered to the grey carpet, leaving him standing there in all his natural glory.

CHAPTER FOUR

NICK froze, embarrassment consuming him. He had an awful feeling it would also shortly consume his natural glory. Linda's wide-eyed staring at his private parts unnerved him totally, especially when he realised they weren't shrinking. Just the opposite, in fact.

If only she would stop looking at him like that!

But she didn't. She kept on looking and he kept on growing. Swiftly. Startlingly.

Nick clenched his teeth down hard in his jaw, shoved Rory into his mother's arms, then bent to sweep the towel up from the carpet. Rewrapping his loins proved somewhat difficult when he found that his hands were shaking.

Anger combined with frustration at this totally alien clumsiness. What in God's name was the matter with him? Fancy letting some female reduce him to this!

'If you've finished gawking,' he snapped, 'I'll go get dressed and be on my way.'

Scowling, he whirled round and stalked back down the hallway and into the bathroom, banging the door behind him. A shave was now off the agenda. He was simply not capable of holding a razor to his throat. He was too angry, both with himself and with her.

'Mug,' he muttered as he began dragging on his clothes. 'Serves you right for playing good Samaritan in the wrong town. City girls don't know how to be

43

grateful, only suspicious. And they have no sense of decorum!'

His anger had cooled somewhat by the time he was fully dressed; the sight of his reflection in the vanity mirror brought a rueful smile to his face. If Madam Linda thought he looked dangerous semi-naked, then wait till she got a load of him like this!

His clean top was black and body-hugging as opposed to his earlier simple white T-shirt. It looked wicked above his tight black jeans, the sleeveless style emphasising the bulging muscles in his arms.

Normally, Nick despised people who judged by appearances, but even he might not have invited the character staring at him in the mirror home for dinner. All that was missing were some tattoos to complete the picture of primitive masculine aggressiveness. An earring or two would not have gone astray as well. Even without those added touches, he could appreciate that he was still far removed from the sort of man a classy woman like Linda would normally associate with.

Not really wanting to scare her half to death, he combed his hair neatly back from his face then dragged his leather jacket on to cover his possibly menacing body. Though, damn it all, she hadn't found a certain part of it menacing a minute or two ago. She'd ogled him like a woman starved of sex.

Which she probably was, came the interesting and provocative realisation. A woman living alone with her baby... Her long-time lover dead... Nothing sexual in her life nowadays but memories.

Hard to live on memories, Nick knew. Eventually, no matter how much you told yourself you would

never look at another member of the opposite sex—
let alone want them—the day invariably dawned when
you did.

Linda was a young woman. Young and healthy and
presumably heterosexual. Had she looked at him just
now and wanted him?

Nick decided he didn't want to know. Dave would
kill him if he touched his precious sister. Hoisting his
rucksack over his shoulder, he swung round and
reached for the doorknob.

Linda paced the family room, trying to quieten the
purple-faced Rory—not to mention her own whirling
thoughts. Her face was still flaming from those
ghastly moments when she hadn't been able to drag
her eyes away from Nick's naked body, her gaze re-
maining riveted to his blatantly male appendages
which had nowhere to hide and which had responded
shamelessly to her ogling.

No, not shamelessly. Nick had obviously been annoyed and embarrassed by his involuntary arousal,
whereas *she* was the one who'd been shameless.
She'd been fascinated then excited by the sheer speed
and power of his erection. He'd looked like an animal,
standing there stark naked with his legs apart. A beautiful, big male animal.

The female animal in her had been stirred, then
challenged by the sight of his obviously unwilling desire. And for a split second she'd wanted him as she'd
wanted no other man—not even Gordon. Her mind
had burned with the image of her going up to him
and touching him; of her doing more than just touching; of her leading him right to the edge till he lost

all control and took her where they were, right there in the hallway.

Rory had somehow disappeared from the scene in her head and she'd imagined Nick dragging her back up and stripping her roughly before pinning her naked and panting up against the wall. He'd imprisoned her hands above her head and prised her legs apart with his before manoeuvring himself into her by then frantic flesh.

He'd moved powerfully within her with deep, voluptuous thrusts, lifting her up onto her toes and propelling her into a previously unknown world where reality receded and she was nothing but a body, searching blindly for release.

Love had nothing to do with her feelings. It wasn't tenderness she sought but passion. And pleasure. Oh, yes, pleasure; a wild, selfish, sweet pleasure which would blot out everything, everything but the feel and smell of him taking her up against a hard, cold wall and making her moan as she had never moaned before.

Her fevered fantasy had been racing towards a monumental climax in her mind when the moment had been shattered by his shoving an unhappy Rory into her arms and stalking off, leaving her to feel totally confused and disorientated.

But when he'd banged the bathroom door behind him, leaving her alone with her suddenly screaming infant, shame had flooded her soul. How could she have entertained such thoughts about such a man? About this stranger. This *bikie!*

He wasn't even her type. She liked her men elegant

and sophisticated. Intelligent and sensitive. Why, next to Gordon, this man was a brute. A beast!

Yet there she'd been a moment ago, lusting after him as she had never lusted before. She could not understand any of it. Her fantasy now appalled her. How could she have wanted to do such things, and to have such things done to her?

Frustration, she decided, desperate to explain the intensity of her desire. It had been nearly two years since she'd had any sex, after all.

Yet, in all honesty, till this very day she hadn't missed the physical side of her relationship with Gordon. It was the man she missed.

She'd never been a highly sexed person. Neither had Gordon, for that matter. Within months of their being together, he would rather have taken photos than make love. Which was why they'd been so well matched. Their love had been based more on companionship and compatibility than a physical passion, had been based on mutual likes and interests. They'd got along. They'd never fought.

Except over her wanting a baby…

Linda sighed a weary sigh while Rory screeched on. Well, she had her baby now, didn't she? And while she adored Rory the feeling didn't seem to be mutual.

Yet he hadn't cried in the arms of that Neanderthal, had he? He'd been as good as gold.

Not like you, a dark voice whispered in her head. You wouldn't be as good as gold in Nick's arms. You'd be everything your mother successfully stopped you growing up to be. A whore. A wanton.

A wild, wicked creature without inhibitions. Or shame.

Linda cringed inside as she recalled that awful day when her mother had walked unexpectedly into the tool-shed down the back yard and found her seven-year-old daughter playing with the eight-year-old boy from next door. He'd been showing her things she'd never seen before when her mother had made her appearance!

Linda's stomach still churned whenever she thought of the scene that had followed. She had not been allowed to play with that boy ever again. And she'd been made to feel so ashamed. And dirty. And disgusting.

She'd grown up being brainwashed into thinking of men and sex as dirty and disgusting. And while her natural intelligence and strong-minded nature had rejected such notions by the time she left school she had certainly never become the most uninhibited female in the lovemaking department.

For one thing, her own satisfaction could only be achieved in the security of a darkened bedroom where the man she was with could not see the contortions on her face. And she was always very, very quiet, making only the softest of noises. A little gasp here. A tiny moan there. On top of that, she had never found the courage to take the initiative. Not for *her* using her hands on a man. Or, God forbid, her mouth!

Which made her fantasy out in that hall all the more shocking. She bitterly resented feeling such outrageous desires for a man she neither loved nor even knew. In fact, it infuriated her, this secret person within herself who had suddenly emerged and could make her want to act in such an uncontrolled and sluttish fashion. She'd always prided herself on never being made to do anything she didn't want to do. But she suspected that if this man ever made a pass at her she would be putty in his hands.

Rory stopped crying abruptly, just in time for her to hear a door opening and shutting out in the hallway.

Linda held her breath. Let him leave. Oh, please just let him leave.

Suddenly, Rory launched forth into another crying jag which almost split Linda's eardrums. The noise stabbed into her brain and she just wanted to scream herself. The door being wrenched open startled her— as did the sight of Nick, dressed now in a chest-hugging black top and a sinfully sexy black leather jacket.

She almost groaned as new and even more outrageous scenarios invaded her mind, none of which took place in the security of a darkened bedroom.

It seemed imperative to say something to distract her new and increasingly perverse imagination. *Anything!*

Attack was always the best defence, she decided in her panic.

'I don't know what you've done to this child of mine,' she began accusingly, her eyes flashing cold fury at him for being able to make her think such wicked thoughts, 'but he just won't stop crying.'

Nick's eyes narrowed as his blood pressure rose. His earlier idea about Linda wanting him sexually—even for a moment—now seemed ludicrous. *Wanted* him?

The only thing this woman wanted to do to him was use him as her whipping boy!

'Now look here, Madam Lash,' he flung back at her. 'I didn't do a damned thing to Rory except look after him. He's over-tired, that's all. Either that, or you're communicating something to his excellent baby antennae which he's finding very upsetting.'

'Like what?' she snapped. 'What are you saying? What are you implying?' Her voice lifted to near hysteria.

Nick could not believe his ears. What was wrong with the woman? Was she paranoid? 'I'm not implying anything! I'm just stating the obvious. You don't have to be a child psychologist to see you have a very unsettling effect on Rory.'

'But I'm his *mother,* for pity's sake. He shouldn't be like this with me all the time. I don't even know what I'm doing wrong!'

Her final words, plus her choked tone, were telling, and carried an unconscious plea for help. Nick sighed and prayed for patience.

'Look, Linda, anyone with a brain in his head can see how tense you are. You're holding Rory way too tightly, for one thing. He's just a baby, not a box of nitroglycerine.' With an air of rueful resignation, Nick dropped his rucksack in the doorway and came to the rescue. Again. 'Here. Give him to me. I'll show you what I mean.'

He swept the little boy out of her arms and flopped him loosely on his left hip. Rory settled immediately, making happy sounds as he started playing with Nick's hair again.

'How did you *do* that?' Linda wailed. 'You're not holding him that much differently to me.'

Nick decided not to pretend he knew it all. His shrug was nonchalant. 'I think my hair helps. Perhaps if you wore yours down you'd have the same effect. He's a bright baby and it gives him something to occupy his mind when you hold him, doesn't it, little fella?' Without thinking anything of it, he gave Rory a kiss on the cheek.

When he looked back at Linda, she was staring at him as though she'd just found out he was a serial killer.

'What?' he said, puzzled.

'Nothing,' she muttered. 'It's just that Rory doesn't usually take to men. He takes one look at Dave and screams blue murder.'

Nick laughed. 'Dave's a devious fellow.'

Linda sighed. 'You could be right. He doesn't like babies much. And he's absolutely hopeless with Rory. Not like you...' Her eyes went from Nick to Rory to Nick again in a type of bewilderment.

'I've had quite a bit of practice,' Nick admitted.

She looked taken aback. 'You have children of your own?'

Nick waited for the wave of pain to crash through him, but surprisingly there was only a small swell of sadness on this occasion. Still, he could not risk exposing himself to those potentially crippling memories by speaking the bitter truth. Old habits died hard.

'Not that I know of,' he said offhandedly. 'But lots of my married friends have babies.'

'You're not married?'

'Nope. I'm not the marrying kind.' Any more.

'Well, I'd better give you your baby back, I think, and get going.'

'Don't go yet!' Linda said abruptly, then looked almost shocked at herself. Nick might have found her reaction amusing if it hadn't been vaguely insulting.

'Would you…um…like some coffee?' she offered—rather nervously, he thought. She'd crossed her arms and was rubbing her hands up and down her upper arms as though she were cold. Yet that could hardly be the case, given the warm weather. 'I was just about to make myself some while I warm up Rory's bottle.'

'Coffee would be great,' he said. 'Black. No sugar. I'll sit and hold Rory while you make it.' He settled himself on the sofa and jiggled a perfectly happy Rory up and down in his lap.

'You're so good with him,' Linda murmured, still in a disbelieving tone. 'Better than Madge, even. Oh, dear Lord, that reminds me. Poor Madge. I hope she's all right. I should ring the hospital and find out how she is. Oh, blast!' she exclaimed with sudden, added agitation.

'What?'

'I have a couple of other phone calls I simply have to make as well. You see, I was planning to have a dinner party tonight and Madge had promised to babysit. But all that's out of the question now, of course.'

Nick bit his tongue to stop himself volunteering to babysit in Madge's place. He knew he wasn't *that* noble, and that this temptation came not from the urge to be of service to his fellow man, but to service his fellow woman!

'But all that can wait till I get Rory his bottle,' she said. 'And our coffee.'

Nick watched while Linda busied herself in the kitchenette behind the bar. It only took him a minute or two to realise that Linda was either the least domesticated female he had ever encountered, or she was nervous in his company. Making them both coffee and Rory a bottle at the same time seemed to stretch her capabilities.

'Oh, botheration!' she muttered irritably when she dropped the teat on the floor and had to get another sterilised one. At one stage she reefed off her jacket and threw it over the back of a chair, revealing surprisingly full breasts, a tiny waist and a nice, trim bottom.

Nick thought how perverse it was that Dave's sister had to be the most attractive female he'd met in donkey's ages. She had everything he liked in a woman. Looks. Intelligence. Class. She even qualified as a career woman.

But he could see she was emotionally vulnerable at the moment. Even if she hadn't been Dave's sister, this would rule her out as a potential sexual partner for him. That, and the ego-deflating fact that she didn't fancy him in return.

Pity, he thought as she walked towards him, carrying a steaming mug in one hand and Rory's bottle in the other. Her breasts swayed enticingly underneath her white shirt, obviously unfettered by a bra. Nick wished it hadn't been quite so long since he'd been with a woman. This was becoming extremely frustrating. He almost regretted not having picked up that blonde in the hotel bar.

'I don't know how you can drink it black with no sugar,' she said as she placed the mug down on a side table near his left arm. 'Here; I'll take Rory now and put him back in his cot.'

'No, don't do that.' Rory was a nice distraction from other disturbing thoughts. 'He can have his bottle here, can't he?'

'What? Oh, yes; yes, I suppose he can.'

Nick lay Rory next to him on the sofa, with a cushion under his head and another by his side to stop him falling off. Rory didn't object, although his eyes never left Nick's. He began pushing the soles of his feet against Nick's thigh while he drank his bottle, the movement much the same as a kitten flexing its paws against its mother's teat while it suckled. It seemed to have a soothing effect on the child, and by the time he was halfway through his bottle he'd fallen fast asleep.

'I don't believe it,' Linda said from where she'd stayed behind the bar to drink her own coffee. 'You really do have an amazing knack with him. Even Madge finds him a handful at times, and she's had three children and five grandchildren of her own.'

'Intelligent children are often a handful,' Nick said. 'They need constant stimulation, yet at the same time a sense of order and discipline. Otherwise they'll run rings around you. Perhaps you should hire a professional to look after Rory while you're at work—someone very experienced with raising all kinds of children.'

'You mean a nanny?'

'A very special nanny, I think, for a very special child.' And Rory *was* special, Nick sensed. A bright little boy who needed a lot of time being spent with him or he would be totally ruined. The last thing he needed was an elderly minder, or to be put into one of those child-care places where there was one carer to an average of seven children. He needed one-on-one care. Since his father had passed away and the mother was clearly emotionally unequipped to handle the child on a twenty-four-hour-a-day basis, then the only choice was a trained professional.

'Can you afford a proper nanny?' he asked. 'The live-in kind?'

'Yes, I suppose so.'

'Then hire one,' he suggested firmly. 'Clearly, Madge won't be on deck for a while. And quite frankly I don't think she's suitable for the job.'

'Really?' came the rather dry remark. Linda straightened and gave him a cold look.

Nick didn't give a damn if she thought him impertinent. Rory's welfare came first. 'Yes, really,' he returned. 'Oh, I'm sure she's done her best but her best is clearly not good enough. Babies like Rory need a firm hand, yet at the same time a lot of love and attention.'

'And you think he'll get that from a paid, impersonal employee?' Linda scoffed.

'What's the alternative? Are you going to give up work and mind him yourself?'

'You think I wouldn't love to do just that?' she flung back at him. 'Do you think I don't feel guilty that I'm a hopeless mother? At least I've had enough honesty and common sense to face my own failings.'

'I don't think you're a hopeless mother,' Nick said, more gently. 'I think you've done very well on such little support. But it's clear you can't manage Rory on your own at this stage. You need professional help.'

Her scowl was black with resentment. 'Thank you for your advice, but, as much as I am grateful for all your help today, I don't think this is any of your business, do you?'

Nick fell broodingly silent. She was right, of course. It wasn't any of his business. But it was extremely difficult not to try to help. Linda and Rory were bringing out his male protective instinct, which normally would have made him run a mile. Emotional involvement of any kind was anathema to him. So why wasn't he running? Why didn't he just get the hell out of here?

'Dave was right,' he muttered.

'Right about what?'

'About your being difficult.'

'Huh! Dave can't point any fingers. Now, I really must make those phone calls. What hospital was Madge taken to, do you know?'

'Saint Vincent's. Private.'

Linda produced a cordless extension from under the counter, plus a directory. She looked up the number and dialled, sounding both surprised and relieved when she was put through to Madge's room.

'Madge, it's Linda!' she exclaimed. 'Oh, it's so good to be able to speak to you. I was so worried. How are you feeling? Have they X-rayed you yet? Is anything broken?'

Nick gleaned from the one-sided conversation that Madge's hip wasn't broken but she was badly bruised. The hospital was also conducting tests on her heart—

probably thinking a dizzy spell caused the fall, Nick concluded.

The conversation finally turned away from Madge's health to Linda's dinner party.

'No, Madge,' Linda said. 'It's out of the question... Who, Nick? Yes, he's still here... No, Madge, I could not possibly ask him. No, Madge,' she insisted strongly, 'it's out of the question!' Her long sigh was expressive. 'Oh, all right, Madge.'

Linda gave Nick a pained glance as she brought the phone over to him. 'Madge insists on speaking to you.' Before she handed over the phone she covered the mouthpiece and whispered, 'Don't take a blind bit of notice of her.'

Nick had an awful feeling he knew what Madge was going to ask him to do. 'Hi there, Madge,' he said into the receiver, hoping against hope that he was wrong. 'No permanent damage?'

'No, the doctor thinks my heart was the problem. Silly man! There's nothing wrong with my heart! I'm just a little overweight. That's why I get puffed out going upstairs, especially when the weather's hot. Anyway, Nick, that's not what I want to talk about. Linda says she's going to cancel her dinner party. *Again*,' she finished with heavy meaning.

'Again?' Nick repeated, glancing up at Linda who was hovering and looking very agitated.

'Is Linda nearby?'

'Yep.'

'I see. Then just listen. Linda has not socialised once since Rory's birth. She never stays to have a drink with her colleagues at the magazine. Or says yes to any of the men who *must* have asked her out.

I appreciate Gordon's death probably shattered her, but life does go on, doesn't it? Still, I'd almost given up hope when suddenly she announced she was going to have a dinner party for some of her friends from work. You could have knocked me over with a feather! But I felt so happy for her. At last, I thought, she's getting it together again.

'Anyway, she was supposed to have this dinner a fortnight ago, but she cancelled at the last minute when Rory got the sniffles. Now she's got another excuse to opt out. I have an awful feeling that if she does that she won't ever invite them again. Lord, they probably won't *agree* to come again. She'll go back into her shell and that will be that.'

'So what do you want me to do?' Nick asked, despite having already accepted the inevitable.

'Please don't let her cancel,' Madge begged. 'You don't really *have* to leave, do you, Nick? I mean, it's not imperative you be somewhere else tonight, is it?'

'No. Not really.'

'Thank God. Will you do it, then? Babysit Rory so Linda won't have any excuse to back out of this dinner a second time?'

'Sure. No trouble.' Nick knew when he was beaten. Besides, if he was honest, he had to admit that he didn't want to leave. Clearly, this unexpected masochism he'd discovered in himself was reaching new heights. Fancy volunteering to mind a problem child along with his problem mother for a whole evening. He wasn't even going to get any sex as a reward!

'I knew you would!' Madge sounded very satisfied with herself. 'You were such a dear to me. I can tell that underneath that rough and tough exterior you're a very soft-hearted fellow.'

'Mmm.' Nick rubbed his still unshaven chin.

'Yes, I understand,' Madge said with conspiratorial softness. 'You can't talk. Now all we have to do is convince Linda. Which might not be quite so easy.'

'I can believe that,' he drawled. Linda was not his greatest fan, unfortunately. She thought he was a bikie bum who'd already severely embarrassed her once today, then had topped it off by spouting his big mouth off on how she should raise her own child.

'Yes, she can be very stubborn, that girl. Perhaps you could play on her sympathetic side. Tell her I'll worry myself sick if I feel I was responsible for spoiling her dinner party. And add that the doctor said worry is the worst thing for me.'

'You mean the silly one who thinks it's your heart?' Nick said drily.

Madge chuckled. 'That's the one. Lay it on thick, Nick. Oh!' She chuckled again. 'I'm a poet and didn't know it!'

Nick could only shake his head. The woman was irrepressible. But such a sweet, generous soul. It was impossible to say no to her.

'Your wish is my command, Madge,' he said. 'You just take it easy, now. Not all doctors are as silly as they sound.'

'Oh, not you too! Now hang up before Linda gets back on this phone and starts arguing with me.'

Nick smiled ruefully. Linda in full argumentative mode was a formidable prospect indeed. 'Okay. Bye, Madge.' He pressed the 'off' button and placed the phone slowly down on a side table.

'She did it, didn't she?' Linda groaned.

'Did what?' Nick said mildly as he glanced up. He knew he was only delaying the explosion, but he rather liked Linda when she simmered. Those lovely blue eyes of hers flashed and glittered. He could almost imagine what they would be like when in the throes of making love.

She crossed her arms and glared at him. 'She persuaded you to stay and babysit Rory for me tonight.'

'Right in one. She also said to tell you she'd be worried sick if she thought she was the cause of your cancelling your dinner, and that worrying was bad for her heart.'

Linda threw up her hands in total exasperation. 'Oh, for pity's sake, you didn't fall for that old chestnut, did you?'

Nick found himself smiling. She really was very desirable when she was angry. 'Can't help it. I'm a sucker for a damsel in distress.'

'I am *not* a damsel in distress!'

'I was talking about Madge.'

Linda pulled a face and began pacing the room, muttering under her breath. Nick thought he heard some not so ladylike expressions.

'Give in gracefully, Linda,' he said. '*I* did.'

She ground to a halt. 'But you don't really want to stay, do you?'

'Oh, I don't know. I've got nothing better to do.'

'I find that hard to believe,' she said tartly. 'Isn't there some leather-clad lady panting for your company somewhere? It *is* Saturday night, after all!'

Nick was taken aback by the savagery of her sarcasm. She sure didn't like him much.

'On top of that,' she raged on, 'I don't want to give this damned dinner party anyway!'

'Why not?'

'Because!'

'Because why?'

'Because I'm not ready for it, that's why!' she snapped. 'Because I don't want to have to smile at people and pretend that…that…'

'That you're not still shattered by Gordon's death?' Nick finished for her.

She stopped and just stared at him. 'How on earth do you know about Gordon? Oh, God—Dave! Dave's been gossiping about me, hasn't he? What's he told you? What else do you know?' Her voice rose to near hysterics.

'Actually, Dave's never mentioned you to me before today,' Nick said calmly. 'And then he didn't say anything of note, other than to say you could be difficult. Madge is the guilty party, I'm afraid. She's quite a talker. Not that I know all that much—only the bare facts. And I have to say I agree with her. You've been very brave, Linda, deciding to have your boyfriend's baby after he was killed. Perhaps too brave. Being too brave has a way of catching up with you in the end.'

'Oh!' she choked out, and then her face began to crumple. 'Oh, God.' And as her hands came up to cover her face she burst into tears.

Nick groaned. Fate wasn't being very kind to him today. With a weary sigh, he rose from the sofa, careful not to disturb the sleeping Rory, and did the only thing the black prince masquerading as a white knight could do to a damsel in distress.

He took her into his arms.

CHAPTER FIVE

SHE felt good. Too good.

Nick exercised a steely control over himself as he endeavoured to go through the motions of white-knight behaviour.

'There, there,' he soothed verbally as he stiffly stroked Linda's back. 'It's all right to cry. Crying's good for you.'

Or so he'd been told. But he'd never been able to, not even when his grief had been at its worst. His hurt had been buried beneath too much hatred. And anger. And guilt.

Eventually, it had been too late to cry.

But he appreciated that it was different for women. They cried far more easily, and often. Sometimes he envied them.

'There, there,' he kept saying, like an automaton, struggling to keep his mind from the full softness of the breasts squashed against his chest and the sensual warmth of her breath against the base of his throat.

Linda knew she was making a complete fool of herself. But she just couldn't help it.

Her tears were not so much caused by recalled grief over Gordon's death but by a sudden and unhappy recognition of her life as it stood that very day. Nick's sympathetic words had really struck deep, especially coming on top of her being so nasty to him. For she hadn't been at all brave in having Rory. She'd been stupid! Having a baby had been a highly emotional and impulsive decision arrived at within days of Gordon's death.

Gordon had promised that he'd give her a baby when they got back to Australia. He'd promised her marriage and an end to their ceaseless wandering of the world. And then he'd gone and got himself killed. Linda's grief had been mixed with anger at Gordon for dying and taking her future away from her. So she'd bullied poor Dave into getting her what she'd thought she wanted, and what she'd hoped would fill the great hole in her heart and her life.

But right from the start it had all gone wrong. She'd been as sick as a dog during her pregnancy, the labour had been horrendous and motherhood a nightmare! Rory made her feel inadequate as a mother and a failure as a female. She hadn't even been able to breastfeed him, although she'd really wanted to.

As if in constant reminder of that failure, her breasts had sprouted from a B-cup to a D-cup and never gone back. All her old bras didn't fit this new, luscious figure and she mostly went around braless. Which was okay in the main, but not right at this moment with their unprotected and sensitive peaks pressed against this man's rock-hard chest.

As her sobs subsided, along with her distress, Linda gradually grew more aware of the strong arms around her and of the smell of the man who owned them. The tang of freshly soaped skin combined with the more exotic scent of leather to send signals to her already dangerously heightened nerve-endings. There was a rush of blood through her veins, sending heat to long-neglected places. Desire, hot and strong, brought the most compelling urges.

The temptation to slide her arms up around his neck was intense. What would he do if she did that? she wondered as her heart raced madly. Would he reject her overtures? Or would he take what was on offer? Then demand more...

Linda knew she was an attractive enough woman, and he'd said he wasn't a marrying man. Looking as he did, he probably had women falling at his feet all the time. Was he indiscriminate with his favours? Was he an unconscionable stud? He looked like a stud. Oh, yes, he *had* to be a stud with that equipment. No male ego could resist wielding such a weapon. And often. She wanted him to wield it with her. She ached for it. God, she was going mad with wanting him. It was sheer torture.

And downright humiliating!

'For pity's sake!' Linda blurted out, and wrenched herself out of his embrace. 'This is just too much, my blubbering all over you as well as everything else! You've already done more than enough,' she said with considerable irony, dashing the remains of her tears from her cheeks and hoping he didn't read anything into her flushed cheeks. 'Please just go, Nick. I can cope by myself. Really I can.'

'Sorry,' he returned with irritating calm. 'Can't do that. I gave Madge my word that I would stay.'

'But Madge need never know!'

'*I'll* know,' Nick said firmly. 'Now, no more nonsense, Linda. You just go and do what you have to do for the dinner tonight, and I'll look after Rory.'

'But...but...'

'But what? What's the big deal? I'll keep out of sight, if you're worried about what your friends might think.'

'It's not that,' she denied swiftly—although, come to think of it, Petra would take one look at Nick and jump to all kinds of conclusions. God, this was getting too complicated for words!

'Then what is it? Is it the dinner party itself? What's the problem? Presumably you've invited friends—no one's going to eat you if everything isn't perfect.'

'No one will probably eat anything,' she muttered in a miserable tone.

'Meaning what?'

Her shoulders sagged and she decided she might as well tell him what else was bothering her. 'I... um...can't cook very well,' she confessed. Gordon had been the cook in their relationship. 'Madge was going to help me.'

'Oh, I see. Is that all? So what were you going to have?'

'Soup and garlic bread, followed by a barbecue and salad, then fresh fruit salad and cream, topped off with a cheese platter and coffee.'

'Sounds pretty basic, Linda. Which parts are worrying you?'

'The meat, mostly. Madge was going to oversee the cooking on the barbecue.'

'I think you'd better forget the barbecue. There's going to be a storm.'

'A storm!' She ran across the room to peer through the glass doors at the sky, where dark clouds from the south were sitting threateningly on the horizon. 'I was going to set the table out on the terrace. Are you sure it's coming this way?'

'No, I'm not sure. But imagine what would happen if it poured buckets out there tonight. Better to be safe than sorry, since you're already a bit uptight about this.'

Linda walked back towards him, crossing her arms again and giving a little shudder. 'I have a feeling tonight is going to be a disaster.' Which might turn out to be the understatement of the year.

'Nonsense. I'll help with the cooking, if you like. I was a short-order cook in a café in Paris once. I'll marinate and grill the meat for you. I'm a dab hand at making salads as well.'

Linda's eyebrows lifted. 'Paris? Really?' She didn't mean to sound sceptical, but Paris had always been reserved in her mind for cultured travellers—not this macho male who had probably never opened a book in his life, let alone visited a museum or the opera.

He gave her a sardonic look, as though he'd read her thoughts and found them almost amusing. She realised he was not remotely what she'd presumed on first sight. Maybe he wasn't an educated man in the strictest sense, but he was definitely street-smart. What he'd said to her earlier about Rory needing a properly trained nanny made a lot of sense. She wouldn't mind having someone else in the house either. It would be nice to have an adult to talk to in the evenings, someone around her own age.

'Yes, Paris,' he repeated drily. 'Believe me when I say I've been around.'

Oh, she believed him. He had a confidently relaxed air which came with loads of experience. She'd bet that those sexy black eyes of his had peered down into plenty of women's faces as they came beneath him. Not for *him* making love in darkness either. He wouldn't want to hide that magnificent body of his.

Linda cursed herself for turning her mind back to sex. But it really was difficult not to think of sex where Nick was concerned. She had never met a more physical man in all her life.

'Somehow I can't see you as a cook,' she told him.

He shrugged, the movement bringing her attention to the broadness of his shoulders. 'I've done hundreds of jobs on my travels. There isn't anything much I can't turn my hand to.'

'Surely there's *something* you can't do!' She just could not get used to the sexual effect he kept having on her, and found some solace in being stroppy.

'I can't produce a great kid like that,' he said, nodding towards Rory before reaching to pick up his coffee once more.

Linda was totally disarmed, and quite moved. What a lovely thing to say!

She smiled softly down at her beautiful baby boy and felt her heart turn over. How could she ever have thought Rory was a mistake? When he was asleep he was an angel. No doubt he would grow out of this difficult phase and prove a delightful child.

'He *is* beautiful, isn't he?' she murmured. 'Not that he takes after me much.' Not for the first time, she wondered who Rory's father was. Maybe one day she'd ask Dave. Meanwhile…

She gave herself a firm mental kick and looked back at Nick, who was frowning slightly as he sipped the last of his coffee. Even frowning he was a most handsome man, and not a Neanderthal at all. It had been very unfair of her to think that. If he had his hair cut, and shaved that stubble off his squared jaw, he might even look civilised. Put a dinner suit on him and he would stop traffic. He probably already did on that bike of his, she thought ruefully.

Their eyes met over the rim of the mug and a shiver ran down Linda's spine. God, but he was sexy!

'By the way,' he said, breaking eye contact as he sat back down on the sofa, careful once more not to disturb Rory, 'if Dave happens to ring tonight for any reason, don't tell him I'm here.'

Linda blinked her surprise. 'Why ever not?'

Nick looked up at her. 'Because he won't approve. He wouldn't even have approved of my mowing your lawn. You see, he doesn't know I did. When he found out I'd spoken to you on the phone he almost blew a gasket, so I told him you were going to get someone else to mow the lawn.'

Linda was utterly thrown. And quite confused. 'But I don't understand. You're best mates, aren't you?'

'We're drinking mates—which is another thing entirely. The cold, hard truth is, Linda, that Dave never told me anything about you because he didn't want me ever to meet you. You see, he considers me a love-'em-and-leave-'em ladies' man, and presumably not a fit person to introduce to his precious kid sister.'

'Oh, really! Anyone would think I couldn't judge a man for myself.' She'd only needed to take one look at Nick to know what type *he* was. 'So *are* you?' she asked, a touch tartly.

'A fit person to be introduced to you?' he asked blandly.

'No—a love-'em-and-leave-'em ladies' man.'

'I wouldn't put it quite like that. The ladies in my life always know the score.'

'Which is?'

'That I'm not a marrying man. That I never fall in love. That I don't want permanency or commitment.'

'That's nothing new,' she said drily. 'Half the men on this planet are like that. And half of the rest are gay!'

Nick laughed. 'Well, that's one trait I don't have. I like women. But you don't have to worry, Linda,' he added. 'I won't make a pass. I steer clear of ladies with babies.'

'How comforting of you to tell me that,' she countered, stung by this last comment. 'And you're quite safe from me too, Nick—I steer clear of blokes on bikes.'

He laughed again. 'Then Dave has nothing to worry about, does he? But I still have a feeling he'd have a hernia if he thought I was here in your house. So we'll keep him in the dark, I think. Now, what about the people coming to dinner?'

'What about them?'

'Do they know Dave?'

'Well, no, not personally. They're just two girls I work with and their partners. They know *of* Dave, but they've never met him.'

'What will you tell them about me?'

Linda just stared at him. 'What do you mean? What about you?'

'Well, if I'm going to help with the meal they're sure to get a few glimpses of me coming and going. A man my size finds it hard to be unobtrusive.'

She tried not to blush as the word 'size' brought back hot memories of seeing him stark naked. 'Yes, well, I can appreciate that,' she muttered. 'I mean... um...' Dear God, what did she mean? She was beginning to lose it again. With a supreme effort of will, she pulled herself together and faced him with a false but hopefully convincing composure. 'I'll just say you're a good friend helping out,' she said swiftly.

'The old "we're only good friends" spiel?' His smile was wry. 'Do you think they'll believe that?'

Linda's own smile was equally wry. She hadn't totally lost her sense of humour. 'I doubt it.'

'Does it matter to you what they think?'

'I suppose so. I have to work with them.'

'In that case you'd better tell them the truth.'

'Which is?'

'That I'm Rory's nanny for the night.'

Linda laughed. Did he have any idea what images would pop into her girlfriends' minds when they took one look at him? He would be assigned various possible roles in Linda's life—and being Rory's nanny was not one of them.

'Okay, okay, I get the picture,' Nick said drily. 'In that case I'll keep out of sight. But you'd better change your mind about the menu. Rather than marinating meat, what you need is a casserole-type meal which can be precooked and just kept hot.'

'Er...can you cook a casserole?'

'No trouble. Provided you've got a well-stocked pantry.'

'Now that is one thing I do have a talent for. I can shop for ingredients like you would not believe! I just don't know how to put them together properly.'

'And I don't think tonight's the night to teach you how,' Nick said in a droll tone. 'Come on, show me where everything is while your little tyrant is off in the land of Nod. Wait! I'll put a couple of chairs up against the edge so that he can't fall on the floor if he rolls over.'

Linda watched in silent awe as Nick made the sofa safe for Rory with brisk, economical movements. He knew just what to do. There was no hesitation. No 'Should I put him in the cot or not?' A decision had been made, followed by the appropriate action.

Linda felt a confusing mixture of resentment and relief. On the one hand, Nick's efficiencies with Rory—and around the house—only highlighted her own wretched inadequacies. On the other hand, it was so good to have someone here who knew exactly what to do. And could do it!

Suddenly, she just wanted to wallow in his competence, to hand over all her problems to him. She would also have liked to return physically to the haven of his arms, to lay her head on the broad expanse of his chest and say, 'Look after me too. Not just Rory.'

It wasn't a sexual thing. It was a desperate need for a temporary sanctuary from the stresses of her life since having Rory. She hadn't realised till that moment how very tired she was, both in body and spirit.

Nick straightened from his task, glanced over his shoulder at her and frowned. 'Are you feeling all right, Linda?'

'What? Yes. Yes, I'm all right.'

He walked over to her, his dark eyes intelligent and intuitive as they gazed down upon her pale face. 'No, you're not. You're exhausted. Look, it's only five. Why don't you lie down and have a nap? I'll take care of things here. I promise I'll wake you up in time for you to dress for dinner.'

'But I can't expect you to mind Rory and cook dinner as well!'

'Not to worry. We'll go to plan B where the dinner is concerned.'

'Plan B?' she echoed blankly.

He smiled. 'I know the owner of an Italian restaurant in Annandale who'll deliver. He owes me one, so it won't be too expensive.'

She opened her mouth to protest again, then closed it, nodding acceptance of his plan B.

Her yawn took her by surprise. So did Nick's hand on her arm. For it was so soft. So gentle. Her eyes met his and her insides contracted.

'Why are you doing all this?' she asked.

'Doing what?'

'Being so nice to me.'

'What a silly question.'

'Is it?'

'Yes. I've already told you I'm a sucker for damsels in distress. Now go and rest while you've got the chance, Linda,' he said, a slight edge in his voice. 'Because this nanny disappears on the stroke of midnight.'

CHAPTER SIX

ONLY a few more hours of being noble, Nick thought testily. It was twenty-five past six, and the weatherman on the news was telling everyone that a fierce electrical storm was approaching Sydney from the south.

'I've got news for you, bud,' Nick muttered. 'It's already arrived.'

A sheet of lightning suddenly lit up the window, and Rory's curly-topped head shot up from where he'd been absorbed playing with some plastic building-blocks on the floor. He'd woken soon after his mother had lain down, and had kept Nick on his toes ever since.

'Don't you dare cry,' Nick warned when he saw that rosebud mouth widen at the rumble of thunder. 'It's just a noise. Big boys don't cry over noises.'

Rory took in Nick's stern tone, decided against crying and returned to his repetitive game of assembling a wobbly pile of bricks then waving his arms around madly till he knocked them over. He squealed with childish delight every time the coloured blocks scattered.

'I can see you're going to be a demolition expert when you grow up,' Nick said when the pile toppled once more.

Rory looked up at him, grinned a gummy grin, then held out his arms to be picked up.

'Not to mention a little con man.' Nick scooped him up and swung him high over his head. The child laughed, his big dark eyes dancing. Nick laughed too—but then a memory suddenly struck of another time and another dark-eyed child. A lump filled his throat and he lowered Rory into his arms, giving him a fierce hug as he buried his face into the child's curls.

'Oh, God,' he groaned. 'God.'

Emotion welled up in his heart and he might have cried for real this time if Rory hadn't twisted his chubby fingers into his hair at that moment and given it an almighty wrench.

'Hell!' Nick exclaimed, his eyes watering with the pain till he managed to disentangle Rory's grip. But pain was exactly what he needed to snap him out of his maudlin state, he decided.

'Time to wake up your mother, I think,' he told Rory, and, plopping him onto his hip, carried him from the room.

Linda was curled up in the middle of the large bed, looking like a little girl. A lock of hair had come loose from its topknot and was lying across her face and mouth. Several strands had worked their way between her softly parted lips and now lay damply against the tip of her tongue. She sighed a soft sigh in her sleep, and that moist pink tongue tip darted forward, pushing the hair aside.

'Damn.' Nick grimaced at the involuntary stirring in his loins, then reached out to shake her abruptly by the shoulder.

'Time to wake up, Linda,' he told her gruffly.

She didn't wake easily, moaning softly as she rolled over and stretched in far too voluptuous a fashion.

Nick gritted his teeth and told himself that this would never happen to him again. The next time he offered his services to a beautiful woman she was going to be unattached, undressed, and under him!

'What time is it?' she asked dreamily.

'Six-thirty,' he snapped.

'Six-thirty!' she gasped, pushing the lock of hair out of her eyes as she sat up. 'Oh, my God, I'll never be ready in time.'

'Of course you will,' Nick pronounced brusquely. 'You have at least an hour before your guests are due to arrive. And people are never early. Just don't dawdle.'

'I never dawdle!' she protested. 'But the table needs setting, and I simply have to wash my hair. It feels as limp as a dish rag with all this humidity.'

'Then I suggest you start with the hair or you'll be greeting your guests with the new wet look. Meanwhile, I'll pop Rory in his cot with a bottle and see what I can do about setting the table. The food hasn't arrived yet, but I'm expecting it shortly.'

'Whatever would I have done without you?' Linda cried as she ran for the bathroom.

'God only knows,' Nick muttered to himself and went about being a good nanny.

'Now you behave yourself for the next hour,' he ordered Rory while he changed his nappy and dressed him in a clean sky-blue terry-towelling jumpsuit. Rory gurgled happily, as though in complete agreement with whatever his new nanny suggested. There wasn't a peep out of him when he was put to bed, though he did immediately kick off his blanket.

'Yes, well, it *is* too hot for blankets just yet,' Nick

conceded. 'But it'll cool down as soon as the rain comes, so I'll be back to cover you up later.'

'Ga-ga,' Rory said.

'Yes, precisely,' Nick said drily. 'I'm going to be gaga before this night is out, I can tell you. Now here's your bottle. Drink it up and off to sleep.'

Nick was a good believer in the saying that the devil made work for idle hands—frankly, Sister Augustine had raised him on it!—so for the next hour he gave the devil a good run for his money. Fortunately, Linda's large and very well laid out kitchen was superbly stocked, so he had little trouble finding the wherewithal to set an elegant dinner table. Just as fortunately, a quick check on Rory around seven showed him sleeping like an angel.

The food arrived shortly after seven, and his old friend had done him proud. For an entrée he'd sent six seafood cocktails, perfectly prepared and ready to serve in shell-like bowls. The main course was well catered for with a huge pot of Gino's special veal and tomato casserole, two bowls of salad and enough crusty herb-and-garlic bread to feed an army.

Dessert was a wide selection of luscious Italian pastries which paid not the slightest attention to the modern trend towards low-fat foods. Gino had even thrown in a couple of bottles of his special vino, the kind that would put a hardened drinker under the table in no time.

On Gino's instructions, the delivery boy would not accept a cent, although Nick did press a twenty-dollar tip into the young man's hands which sent him away whistling.

Nick immediately put the entrées and dessert in the

fridge, and the main course in the oven. He hid the wine in a bottom cupboard—he didn't think Linda and her guests were ready for Gino's potent brew— then began opening a couple of bottles of the more suitable white wine which he'd found chilling in the fridge door.

An extra-loud crash of thunder suddenly rocked the house, and Nick grimaced. If that didn't wake Rory he didn't know what would. He stopped what he was doing and dashed upstairs, only to find the door to Rory's room already open.

Nick tried not to do a double take at the sight which met him as he moved into the open doorway. But the Linda peering over the side of Rory's surprisingly quiet cot was not the same as the Linda who'd scrambled off her bed nearly an hour before. Even when she'd had her hair up, no make-up on and her woman's body housed in less than feminine clothes, Nick had found her extremely attractive.

His eyes now moved disbelievingly over the silken length of honey-brown hair which flowed in glossy abandonment halfway down her back. The androgynous navy trousers and white shirt had been discarded in favour of something long and slender and red.

She glanced up at his abrupt arrival, and he swallowed convulsively. Dear God, help me...

She was just so lovely. And so damned desirable. Her mouth was as scarlet as her dress. Her eyes were dark-rimmed and alluring. And that hair...

He must have masked his lust well, for she showed no alarm as her eyes met his. 'Shh,' she whispered, and began walking towards him. 'Don't wake him.'

Nick swallowed again.

It wasn't a dress she was wearing—it was a skirt and matching vest. The skirt hugged her hips then swirled out around her ankles. The vest outlined her hourglass figure, swelling out at her breasts before curving in at her tiny waist. Four gold buttons winked their way from between her breasts down to her waist. More gold swung from her ears. She looked like a wild gypsy princess, and he ached to ravage her on the spot.

Instead he stepped back out of the doorway, balling his fists in frustration while she came out and carefully closed the door. Even with his back pressed against the wall, he was still close enough to be assailed by the perfume that wafted from her body. Nick loved perfume on a woman, especially the type Linda was wearing tonight—musky and exotic and sinfully expensive.

'Rory's a good sleeper at night, but I was sure the thunder would have woken him,' she said, smiling at Nick as she turned to face him.

He ruefully recalled the expression on her face when they'd first met in this hallway and decided it was much safer when she was scowling at him, not smiling.

'Well, you have to be lucky sometimes,' he muttered in total self-mockery. 'Now, if you're ready, we'd better go downstairs and I'll explain the menu.'

'The food arrived, then?'

'It did. And, before we have an argument over the bill, Gino wouldn't accept any money so you don't owe me a thing. Now, I've put the cold courses in the fridge and the hot in the oven,' he said as he strode off in the direction of the stairs, Linda scurrying after him. 'You shouldn't have any trouble serving any of it. And, for pity's sake, there's no need to tell your friends the truth. Let them think you're a culinary genius.'

'But this is all simply wonderful!' Linda exclaimed a few minutes later. 'And you've set the table as well!' she gushed, on sliding the door back which separated the kitchen from the dining area. 'And so beautifully! Oh, Nick, how am I ever going to be able to thank you?'

Several suggestions came to mind, all of which he didn't think Linda would go for.

'There's no need,' he said in one hopefully final display of heroic gallantry. 'It was my pleasure entirely.'

Her sudden colouring surprised him. What had he said to embarrass her? She glanced agitatedly away from his frowning gaze, one of her hands fluttering up to fill the deep V of her neckline, as though she was trying to hide the flush of her skin.

'Linda? What is it? What did I say?'

'Nothing,' she said, her eyes fixed at some distant spot in the dining room. 'I...I'm just ashamed of myself, that's all.'

'But why? What for?'

Her eyes swung back to his, anxious and glittering. 'What for? For a lot of things, but mostly for being so rude to you when I first came home. And for misjudging you.'

'Misjudging me?'

'Yes. Just because you ride a motorbike and dress the way you do I assumed you were some kind of mindless, macho Neanderthal—where as in fact you're a very intelligent and extremely kind man with more know-how and common sense than most of the supposedly professional men I've known! I also feel ashamed of asking you to stay upstairs and hide while I serve this wonderful food which *you've* provided to a group of people I don't really give a damn about. I wish I'd never invited them. I wish...I wish...'

The doorbell rang and Linda groaned. Suddenly, she seemed in danger of a very serious stress overload.

'Linda, calm down,' Nick advised firmly. 'I promise you I didn't take offence at any of your reactions today. They were entirely understandable. There's no need for you to feel ashamed or guilty over anything.'

At this she looked even more pained, so Nick took another tack. 'Look, you've had a difficult time lately and today would have been enough to rock anyone's socks. I'm just glad I was able to be of some help. Now, go let your friends in and enjoy your evening. If you feel really guilty about the food then bring some up to me,' he added. 'I am a mite hungry, and I have a wicked penchant for Gino's veal casserole. A couple of those pastries in the fridge wouldn't go astray either. Fair enough?'

She just shook her head at him. 'You make it all sound very simple, but it isn't.'

'It can be if you want it to be.'

She cocked her head on one side, her eyes searching his in a bemused fashion. 'You just don't understand, do you? But how could you?'

The doorbell rang again, sounding insistent this time.

'I understand that if you don't answer that soon Rory might wake up,' Nick warned.

She sighed. 'All right, I'm going. I know when I'm beaten.'

'And so do I,' Nick muttered, dashing away upstairs before Linda had another fit of the guilts and asked him to stay and eat downstairs. The last thing he needed was a few more hours of her unnerving presence, especially now that she'd decided he *was* a white knight, and not the black prince.

Little did she know that she'd been right the first time. She hadn't misjudged him totally. Over the last ten years he'd acted the role of mindless, macho Neanderthal with more women than he could count!

And, while he'd embraced a noble gallantry today instead of his usual male chauvinism, he rather suspected it wouldn't take much to tip the balance of the scales back the other way. He also suspected that the evening ahead might still test his gallantry further, and so he braced himself for the fray.

When Linda popped upstairs at regular intervals, both to check on Rory and to bring Nick each course of the meal, he was ready with a suitably cool mask in place, keeping the television on and pretending to be absorbed in the none too scintillating Saturday evening programmes. Even so, each time she lingered far too long for his peace of mind and body, and he heaved a great sigh of relief at each exit.

His frustration was taken to new heights when she brought him coffee around ten and stayed even longer than before, first sitting on the arm-rest of the sofa and chatting away, before wandering across the room and standing at the window to watch the storm, which had finally hit with full force. Rain lashed the glass and branches of trees brushed the guttering under the force of the wind.

Nick found her just as disturbingly desirable with her back towards him. He kept looking at her hair and wanting to twist it around his fingers and drag her back down onto the sofa with him; wanted to slide his hands up under that vest and over her naked breasts; wanted to have her squirming and panting beneath him.

'For pity's sake, Linda,' he finally snapped. 'What will your guests be thinking, with your disappearing up here all the time?'

Linda turned, her arms crossing defensively over her breasts, her expression rebellious. 'I don't really care what they think. I've never been so bored in all my life. I thought it would do me good to have some people over, to have some adult conversation and company, but it hasn't worked out that way. I mistakenly imagined Petra and Louise were friends, but I can see they don't care about me any more than I care about them.

'I told them what happened to Madge and they weren't even interested enough to ask how she is, or what I'm going to do on Monday about work. And since Rory is safely in bed he doesn't even exist in their eyes. Louise even said contemptuously that she has no intention of ever having children and spoiling *her* figure. Petra agreed wholeheartedly. As for their boyfriends... All I can say is if that's all that's on offer if I re-enter the dating game then thank you, but no, thanks!'

Nick was startled by her outburst, but he empathised with everything she'd said. She'd just echoed what he'd found himself in the singles world these past ten years. Not that he'd been looking for a partner. He hadn't. But he could not help noticing the lie of the land when it came to relationships these days, and could well understand Linda's disillusionment.

Most of the heterosexual single people over thirty were hopelessly screwed up, chronically selfish and ridiculously demanding. Their expectations were unrealistically high. They wanted it all but weren't prepared to give much. Compromise was a no-no. Sacrifice was unheard of. And commitment lasted only as long as that first flush of passion, which usually hit the wall pretty quickly once the relationship moved from the initial fantasy phase to the tougher going of day-to-day life.

'Relationships are very complicated these days,' Nick commented. 'Good ones are rare.'

She frowned over at him. 'Is that why you don't have any?'

'Partly.'

'And what's the other part?'

Nick was shocked at how tempted he was to tell her, to sit her down and pour out everything. But what would that prove? Would it bring Sarah and Jenny back to him? Would it change a single, damned rotten detail of the past?

It would only upset him all over again, was his age-old excuse for keeping silent.

Yet Sister Augustine and that doctor had both said he should talk about his loss and his grief. They'd said that was the only way to get rid of the anger and the guilt. Nick hadn't believed them.

Now he wondered if they'd been right...

He stared at Linda and simply ached to unburden himself. She would be compassionate, he knew. She might even come close to understanding how he'd felt, and still felt. She too had lost someone in tragic circumstances.

He marvelled again at her bravery in deciding to have her lover's baby after he'd been killed. Surely every time she looked at Rory she must think of his father?

Maybe that was part of her problem in her bonding with the child. Did she subconsciously resent Rory's being alive when the man she loved was dead? Did she feel guilty over still being alive herself? Maybe she felt she should have died with him.

Nick had felt that. He'd briefly wanted to die. To enable him to go on, he'd embraced the burning power of revenge for a while. But when he'd finally been awarded that huge compensation payment in the courts he'd suddenly seen the folly of his ways. Revenge held no lasting triumph or satisfaction. The anger and guilt were still there, and the money meant nothing to him.

So he'd left it all behind and run. Run from the pain. Run from the loneliness. Run from the brutal reality of still being alive when all he'd loved and promised to protect was dead.

And the running had worked to a degree. Time and the constant travel—the distraction of different places, different jobs and different people—had healed the rawest of his wounds. He could even function pretty normally.

But marriage and another family was something he

didn't even contemplate. So he always kept his friendships and relationships with women very superficial and strictly sexual.

So why the hell did he yearn to draw *this* woman close to his heart? He could understand his wanting to sleep with her. Any red-blooded man would want that. But to unburden his soul? To risk an emotional involvement? She was the last woman he'd want to fall in love with. She had a child, goddammit. She was looking for a man to share her life with, not a fly-by-night hellraiser whose only want in life now was to live each day as it came with no thought of tomorrow, let alone permanent responsibility.

Hell, he should be running a mile instead of looking at her now and coveting not only her body but also her woman's warmth and compassion.

Then why aren't you, you mug? he asked himself.

'I think you'd better go back downstairs,' he suggested firmly in a vain attempt at being sensible. 'Your guests will be wondering where you are.'

'Then let them wonder!' she snapped. 'If I go back down I'll only drink far too much wine and give myself a headache trying to find things to say. The four of them are perfectly content cuddling up to each other, anyway. They've been all over each other like rashes since they arrived. I don't know why they bothered to come. A few minutes ago I almost told them not to worry about the meal or me, to just get down on the floor and get right on with it.'

Nick smiled a rueful smile. It seemed dear Linda had been having as frustrating an evening as he'd been. 'Why didn't you?' he mocked.

'I wish I had.' She sighed an irritable sigh. 'Don't

you think it's a pity that you can never say exactly what you're thinking? Wouldn't you like to just say it as it is sometimes, without fear or favour?'

'Absolutely. But unfortunately, in the main, telling the bare truth gets you into trouble.' He could just imagine what she'd say if he told her that right at this moment he wanted to take off all her clothes and get *her* down on the floor!

'Tell me what *you're* thinking,' she ordered him suddenly. 'Right at this moment. I want the truth, the whole truth and nothing but the truth.'

'No, you don't,' he mocked.

'Yes, I do,' she countered, tossing her head defiantly, the action sending her earrings swinging and her hair shimmering like silk.

There was no denying the flirtatious flavour in her words and her actions. Or Nick's surprised realisation that Dave's sister was actually making an oblique pass at him.

His narrowed gaze carried a new and penetrating thoughtfulness as it travelled down her body then up again. He noted the rapid rise and fall of her breasts, the peaked nipples, the flush in her cheeks.

Well, blow me down, he thought.

The very real possibility that she might want him as much as he wanted her swiftly obliterated any concern over an unwise involvement, sexual or otherwise. Even the sudden guilty expression on her face did nothing to sway him from his new resolve. He rose to his feet and walked inexorably towards her, holding her with his eyes, telling her with his own visual hunger what he had in mind.

He half expected her to bolt for the door. But she

didn't. She stayed, staring up at him, her eyes wide and unblinking, like those of a rabbit trapped in the headlights of a car.

And that car was coming straight towards her with all its dangerously lethal power.

When Nick stopped at arm's length from her body and reached out to tip her chin up with a single, firm fingertip, he felt her tremble right down to her toes. It was not a tremble of fear, he believed, but of intense excitement. He could see the hunger in her glittering eyes, and the way her lips had fallen apart so that she could suck more air into her panting lungs.

And he relished every telling detail.

'You want to know what I'm thinking?' he taunted softly, his finger tracing down her throat then down into the deep V of her neckline. 'I'm thinking that you're in desperate need of a man. And I'm just the man to accommodate you.'

Her lips parted further in shock, and he was about to kiss them when there was a blinding zigzag of lightning outside, followed by an immediate and cataclysmic crash of thunder. The lights and the television went off, plunging the room into darkness.

CHAPTER SEVEN

LINDA gasped, then groaned when she felt Nick's finger lift from her flesh. He was stopping. That was all she could think about at that moment. The blackout didn't matter. Neither did her visitors downstairs. He was *stopping!*

She groaned again. She didn't want Nick to stop. She wanted him to take her in his arms, wanted him to touch her, kiss her, undress her. Yes, he was so right—she was desperate for a man.

But not any man. Just Nick.

She wanted to do everything with him, everything she'd been taught to think of as indecent and shameful. She wanted him to strip away all her inhibitions, as well as her clothes. She wanted to put aside the strait-laced Linda who had inhabited her body for the past thirty-odd years and embrace a new Linda, the Linda which had emerged the moment she'd seen Nick standing naked before her this afternoon. *That* Linda had known instinctively what she'd wanted, with no shame and no qualms.

And, while the brainwashed Linda had battled to suppress this bolder side of herself, she could see now that this new and more exciting Linda had kept a subtly controlling hand this evening. She'd directed her choice of clothes, the way she'd done her hair, the perfume she'd chosen to wear.

Wear? Good God, she'd practically *bathed* in the

stuff. There wasn't a secret fold or pore in her body which didn't reek of Opium.

And then there'd been her behaviour tonight. In the past, she'd always been pretty cool and standoffish in her dealings with men. She never gave them an inch. Gordon had even accused her of becoming a feminist.

But with Nick she'd suddenly discovered a far more feminine side, indulging in apologies, flattery, gratitude and servitude. She hadn't been able to stay away from him for more than ten minutes at a time, running upstairs at every excuse just so that she could look at him, be with him and talk to him.

With each visit upstairs she'd become just a little more desperate to attract his sexual interest, till finally she'd been reduced to flirting and Nick had seen the light behind her uncharacteristic behaviour—had seen it and decided to act on it with a darkly merciless resolve which had sent her already dangerously aroused body into overdrive.

And, while she'd been rather surprised by the presumptuously arrogant way he'd taken control of things, she could not have stopped him in a million years.

She didn't want him to stop now.

'We'll have to put this on hold,' Nick muttered into the darkness. 'You go see if Rory's woken up and I'll get rid of your visitors. Do you have a torch up here anywhere?'

'No, I don't,' she replied rather breathlessly. 'There *are* some candles and matches downstairs in the kitchen.'

'I know; I saw them earlier. But we're not going to disclose that fact to your visitors, are we? We're not going to admit to having any other lights of any kind at all.'

'But...'

He gripped her shoulders and she could just make out his face as her eyes grew used to the darkness. 'Do you want me to get rid of those people or not, Linda?' he asked sharply. 'Is this your way of telling me you've changed your mind?'

'No...'

'You don't sound very sure.'

She didn't know what to say. Her earlier, mad desires had been dampened a little by the interruption to the proceedings. And some embarrassment was creeping in. What must he think of her? As much as she yearned to be more sexually adventurous, she despised people who indulged in tacky one-night stands. 'I...I just don't want you to think I'm cheap,' she said.

'For pity's sake, Linda, what decade were you born in? I don't think a woman is cheap because she acts and feels like a normal, heathy female. Cheap has nothing to do with sex and everything to do with a person's all-round character. You could never be cheap. Never!'

She flushed with pleasure at his impassioned words. They made her feel a lot better.

'Now that we've got that settled,' Nick went on brusquely, 'just do as I say, okay? Here. Take this.' And he produced a tiny light from his pocket which, when handed over, Linda saw was a miniature lantern attached to a set of keys.

'It turns on and off by twisting the base.' He

showed her. 'It runs on a tiny battery, so don't leave it on indefinitely.'

'Oh, how cute! But won't you need it to go downstairs?'

'I have a pencil torch in my rucksack. Now, I want you to promise me not to come downstairs. I'm going to tell them Rory has woken and is very upset by the storm. Once they see there's nothing more for them to do except sit in the darkness by themselves, they'll take my suggestion and leave.'

'You don't think they'll be offended?'

'Not in the slightest. From what you've said they'll be only too happy to go home and screw themselves silly.'

Linda winced. She hated the word 'screw.' It was so hard and cold. Was that how Nick would think of sex with her? That he was screwing her silly?

'I'll go down now,' Nick said. 'And remember what I told you. Don't come downstairs. Not till you hear their cars drive off, anyway.'

Linda took a few seconds to gather herself after Nick's departure. Then she hurried along to Rory's room. She didn't think he could have woken or he would surely have been crying.

Blessed silence met her when she opened the door, and, while she was relieved, Linda wasn't really surprised. Rory could be a terror during the day, hardly napping at all, but once he went to sleep at night wild horses would not wake him.

Linda's heart welled up with love for her son as she looked down at his angelic, sleeping face. She determined to be a better mother in future, to try to be more relaxed with him, as Nick had suggested.

And she would move heaven and earth to find the very best nanny to look after him. She would not go back to work till she had.

This thought brought a worried frown to her face. Next month's magazine went to press this Friday. As the features editor it was crucial that she be there this week. If she let them down she just might not have a job to go back to. Although Gordon had left her well provided for with a house, contents and car, there was not a lot of actual cash left in the bank. She *needed* her job. And she needed to work. It was no use pretending otherwise. She'd tried being a twenty-four-hour-a-day mother and she'd almost gone barmy!

Sighing, Linda put the little lantern keyring down on the dressing table and tucked the blanket firmly back around her son.

'But don't you worry, my darling,' she whispered, and transferred a kiss from her fingers to his forehead. 'That's Mummy's problem. I'll work something out tomorrow. Maybe they'll let me bring you into work with me.'

Picking up the little lantern and keys, she tiptoed from the room, switching off the light once she was back out in the hallway. She used the wall to guide her along to the top of the stairs, where she sat on the step in the darkness and listened with interest as Nick shepherded the two couples across the foyer and through the front door.

'Linda sends her apologies and says she'll ring you,' Nick was saying briskly. 'Thank you for coming. Watch yourself on those steps. Bye, now.'

Linda shook her head. Not a protest or a peep out of any of them. It seemed Nick was right. Either that or they'd been struck speechless by the sudden appearance of a macho giant in black coming down the stairs and ushering them out of the house.

Nick did have an overpowering persona and presence, Linda conceded.

She heard him close the front door, then heard him sigh. It was an odd sigh. Not weary, but troubled-sounding.

Had *he* changed his mind? came the instant, panicky thought. Didn't he want to sleep with her any more? Was he worried that she might not know the score, as was required by all his transitory lady-friends?

The thought that he might just turn around and leave sent her jumping to her feet.

'Nick!' she cried out.

'What? What is it?' He bounded up the stairs and shone the pencil of light into her face.

'You…you weren't going to leave too, were you?'

'Leave? Why would I do that?'

'Because…well…you might think that I was one of those ladies with babies who's on the lookout for a man not just for a night but for life.'

'That thought hadn't occurred to me,' he said. '*Are* you?'

'No, of course not! I just want you to…to…'

'Quite,' he said.

She was confounded by the sharp edge in his voice. 'But isn't that what you want too, Nick?'

His hesitation to answer confused her all the more. 'Nick?'

'Yes, of course,' he said impatiently. 'Now, let's go and light some candles before this torch battery gives out. Which reminds me—where are my keys? I don't want to lose them. Can't get Old Faithful going without them.'

So he *was* already thinking of leaving, Linda thought unhappily. The image of him indulging in a five-minute quickie with her before roaring off on his motorbike was depressing in the extreme.

She silently handed over the keys, which he pushed into his jeans back pocket.

'Right,' he said. 'Give me your hand. This torch is fading fast, and the last thing I want is you falling down these stairs and ending up in the bed next to Madge.

'So how was Rory?' he asked as he drew her carefully down the stairs, only a thin beam of light showing the way. 'I didn't hear anything, so hopefully he stayed asleep.'

'Yes, he did. He's a good sleeper at night. Nothing much wakes him after nine.'

'You've no idea how glad I am to hear that.'

He gave her hand an intimate squeeze and her heart fluttered wildly. The possibility that he might spend the whole night with her if she asked sent a ripple of delight quivering all the way down her spine.

'Nick,' she said, pulling him to a halt as they reached the bottom of the stairs.

He directed the beam right into her face. 'Yes?'

The curt wariness in his voice caused her courage to fade. If she asked him to stay the whole night, he might interpret that as her already making demands on him—as her being one of those women who clung and wanted more than he was prepared to give.

'Were...were Petra and company annoyed about your asking them to leave?' she asked instead.

Nick gave a short, dry laugh. 'You've got to be joking. I think they were relieved. Look, Linda, get real. They probably only came to get a free feed. And they'd already had that, hadn't they?'

'Oh! What a cynical thing to say!'

'Sorry, but I *am* cynical. So are you, if you're truthful. We've both reached the cynical thirties.'

Linda was about to voice a protest when she pulled herself up short. Nick was right. She *had* become more cynical over the past year or so. Gordon's death had stripped her of his protective presence then propelled her into the real world with a vengeance.

Unfortunately, she hadn't realised that at the time, and had plunged into her decision to have Rory before cold, hard reality had sunk in. Like a lot of girls these days, she'd had a tendency to coat the idea of single motherhood with a romantic glow. She'd also stupidly embraced the modern female belief that she could do and be everything at the same time.

Linda now knew from firsthand experience that she was not Superwoman. She also wasn't totally self-sufficient. She needed support.

And above all, surprisingly, she needed Nick.

'Come on.' Nick tugged her hand. 'Let's go get those candles.'

'Exactly how old *are* you, Nick?' she asked on their way to the kitchen.

'Thirty-five.'

'You look younger.'

'So do you.'

'Well, I hope so,' she laughed. 'I'm only thirty-one.'

'I meant younger than thirty-one. Dave told me your age.'

She was startled. 'I think Dave told you more about me than you've admitted.' Thank God, though, her big-mouthed brother hadn't mentioned Rory's unconventional conception. She rather liked Nick's admiration of her so-called bravery in having Gordon's baby. If he knew the truth, he would look upon her as if she was a fool—a silly, naive, self-indulgent fool!

'I dragged a few basic details out of him after your phone call, that's all. Ah, here's the drawer with the candles and matches.'

He placed the ailing torch on the counter and drew a long white candle out of the full box. Once it was lit, they were both immediately bathed in a circle of golden light much more atmospheric than the torch. It cast ghostly shadows upon Nick's face and added a menacing edge to his harshly handsome features, highlighting his five o'clock shadow and the black depths of his deeply set eyes.

Linda's eyes drifted down his equally menacing body—his powerful chest was encased in black, while his long, muscular arms were bare. She swallowed as her imagination filled with the most spellbinding fantasies.

She was so engrossed in looking at him and thinking hot thoughts that she gasped when he reached out to touch her cheek. 'A penny for your thoughts?'

She shivered at the thought of exposing her secret

desires to him. 'It would take much more than a penny to pry them out of me,' she choked out.

He laughed softly, then fell silent as he held the candle closer to her face. She could feel the heat of the flame against her skin. Or was it her own heat burning her cheeks?

'You are one beautiful woman,' he murmured, his fingers travelling all over her face as though he were a blind man reading her features with his fingertips. 'This one little candle is just not going to do,' he said in a low, almost hypnotic voice as he moved his fingertips back and forth across her mouth. 'Do you have any candlesticks anywhere?'

'In…in the music room,' she whispered shakily through those galvanising, tantalising fingertips. They felt like the skin of ripe peaches against her lips. She ached to kiss them, lick them, suck them.

But she just could not bring herself to.

The thought that she might be shrinking back into that old Linda who would cringe at anything but the missionary position in a darkened bedroom demoralised her totally.

She quivered uncontrollably when one of his fingertips brushed against the tip of her tongue. At least she could mindlessly enjoy what *he* did to her. That was something.

She almost moaned when his hand dropped away.

'Take me there,' he said.

The moment was broken, her escalating desires left hanging in the air. Linda felt disorientated, and acutely dismayed. She had great difficulty gathering herself together.

'Down this way,' she said stiffly. 'Give me that candle. And bring three more.'

Linda took the lit candle from his hands and walked down to the door at the other end of the galley-style kitchen. Presumably, Nick hadn't been in this part of the house. Why would he have been? She didn't come in here herself all that much. It depressed her.

'This was Gordon's favourite room,' she said as she went in, then waited for the depression—and possibly the guilt—to hit. Gordon would have been truly shocked by what she was doing. He'd been very strait-laced about sex. She was pretty shocked at herself!

'Over here,' she said tautly, and crossed the room to where a sleek, shiny baby grand piano rested under the large window overlooking the terrace. Sitting on top was a three-pronged crystal candelabrum which she'd bought in Italy. It had been relatively cheap and Gordon had criticised her over the purchase, saying it was poor-quality crystal. Yet when they'd returned home he'd put it in pride of place on his piano and had taken credit for the buy whenever anyone had complimented him on it.

'Nice-looking piano,' Nick commented on joining her. 'Do you play?'

'No. Neither did Gordon. But he liked quality things. This was said to be the best money could buy.'

Nick bent to peer at the German brand name. 'It certainly is,' he said.

Linda frowned. 'You know something about pianos?'

'A little.'

'You mean you actually *play?*'

His smile was wry, and she knew she'd done it again: misjudged him.

'Occasionally,' was all he said, but Linda felt terrible. She must have offended him, and that was the last thing in the world she wanted to do.

'Will...will you play something for me?' she asked, in an attempt at reparation.

'No,' he said, quite calmly, and lifted the heavy candelabrum carefully down onto the keyboard lid. 'Perhaps some other time. I have other things I'd rather be doing at this moment.' He gave her a hard yet highly sensual look over his shoulder, and she fairly quaked inside.

At last he dropped his eyes back to the candelabrum and started attending to the task in hand. Linda found her gaze riveted to his hands as they screwed the first candle deep into its holder. Was he really doing it as slowly and as deliberately as it seemed? And with such erotic suggestiveness? Her mouth went dry when he repeated the procedure with the second candle. When he really rammed the third one in she made a small, choking sound.

His eyes jerked up to take in her flushed face, and she just knew that he knew what she'd been thinking and feeling.

'Come closer.'

She trembled inside at the command in his voice. And the almost icy control. Why was it, she wondered, that she found his control so exciting? Was it because she herself was spinning way out of control?

There was no question of not obeying him. There was such a sweet, dark pleasure in placing herself totally in his hands. She revelled in the mixture of fear and excitement which rushed through her veins as she crossed the distance between them.

Yes, she was afraid of him, afraid of what he might do to her. Yet underneath, on some other, instinctive level, she trusted him implicitly not to actually hurt her but to take her to places she would never dare to go on her own. There was a whole world of delicious pleasures out there that she had never tasted. And she wanted him to make her taste them tonight.

She moved to stand a breath away from him, expectant and helplessly turned on. Every nerve-ending in her body felt electrified. Her nipples were hard against the satin lining of her vest. Her whole breasts felt swollen. There was a churning deep in her stomach, along with an exquisite tension.

She sucked in a sharp breath when he reached up to encircle her wrist, but all he did was tip the candle she was holding over on its side and direct its flame to the wicks of the three candles in the candelabrum. When they were lit, he let her go and lifted the candelabrum high.

'Follow me,' he ordered, and he headed back through the kitchen.

She did, like some programmed robot.

But a robot did not have a pounding heart, or endless knots in its stomach. A robot's face did not flame wildly at the thought of what was ahead of it.

Only in her blind obedience was she a robot.

She followed him down the length of the kitchen and into the dining room, where the long glass table was still strewn with dirty plates, half-empty coffee-cups and empty wineglasses. It seemed a strange place to take her, she thought dazedly. But a robot didn't question. It just obeyed.

He bent and placed the candelabrum under the table, the candles sending an unearthly glow up through the glass. Then he walked down each side of the table, sweeping all before him with an outstretched arm, piling everything up in an untidy jumble at the far end.

His actions reminded her of an erotic scene from a famous movie which took place on a large kitchen table. She went hot all over just thinking about it. Surely he didn't mean to do anything like *that?* She shivered violently as she stared down at the table, which looked like a pagan altar with those three candles glowing underneath it.

'You can't possibly be cold,' Nick whispered from just behind her.

Her heart leapt and she dropped the candle she'd been holding. It clattered onto the polished floor and rolled away, the wick snuffing out.

'I…you…you frightened me,' she rasped, spinning round to face him.

'Would I do that?' he murmured.

She gasped again when he suddenly scooped her up and sat her on the edge of the table.

'What…what are you doing?' she protested breathily.

'Exactly what you want me to do,' he said. 'So hush up, lovely Linda, and just enjoy.'

'But…but…'

His kiss silenced her, then did so much more. It brought forth that new Linda again, the one who would never protest or shrink back, the one who instantly wallowed in the hot invasion of his tongue in her mouth, and at the same time quickly yearned for other invasions. She moaned a deeply sensual moan, slid her hands up into his hair and told him with her own tongue that she would go wherever he led, and do whatever he wanted.

CHAPTER EIGHT

SWEET Lord, Nick thought when Linda started kissing him back. He'd known some passionate women in his day, but she left the others in the shade. She was on fire, a volcano ready to erupt.

Nick was pretty close to erupting himself!

He had to distance himself from her heat fairly quickly or he wouldn't have a hope in Hades of giving her what she obviously wanted and needed. Once was not going to be enough.

There again, once wasn't going to be enough for him, either. He wanted this night to last as long as possible. So he set about cooling his dangerously aroused body by concentrating on *her* pleasure rather than his, by focusing all his attention on finding out exactly what turned her on the most, what she liked above all else.

Till a moment ago, he'd thought she favoured playing the submissive female to his dominant male. Most women did. But he could see now that she would relish taking the assertive role as well when the time was right.

He aimed to make sure the time *was* right sometime during the coming hours. But when the lovemaking was finally over, when the fires had been extinguished for both of them, he aimed to walk away. Oh, yes. There would be no repeat performance at some future date, Nick vowed staunchly. No offering his services to the far too needy and greedy Linda a second time. When the dawn came, he would be well gone, never to return.

Linda moaned when he cupped her face and started easing his mouth from hers. She dug her fingertips into his scalp and tried to force him back, but he took her hands by her wrists and pressed them palm down against the glass table on either side of her. Her splayed fingers automatically curled over the edge.

'Now keep them there,' he commanded curtly. 'And sit still.'

She kept them there and sat still, eyes blinking wide when he pushed her skirt up over her knees, exposing her bare legs and her thighs. She stared, dry-mouthed and heart pounding, when he picked up her left ankle and began unbuckling the strap of her black sandal. He slipped the shoe from her foot then let it fall softly to the floor before doing the same to her other foot.

On the surface they were simple, straightforward actions yet, somehow, the nakedness of her legs brought an acute sexual awareness which turned every touch into the most sensually erotic caress. She quivered with each brush of his fingers, her toes curling over in an echo of the curling sensations in her stomach.

'You have lovely legs,' he murmured, before parting those legs and standing between them.

Her heart began to thud heavily, blood pounding in her temples. She gulped when he started undoing the buttons on her vest with quick, skilful fingers. In seconds he was peeling the two sides apart, revealing her aching, aroused breasts.

She held her breath when he began stroking over them oh, so gently with his hands. Her nipples peaked hard beneath the heat of his palms, sending flames of fire through her breasts and down to that area between her thighs already burning for him. When he started rolling the sensitive peaks with his thumb-pads, she squeezed her eyes tightly shut and automatically arched her back.

He swiftly satisfied her silent plea, taking first one swollen nipple then the other into his hot, wet mouth. His tongue teased, then his teeth tormented till she was panting her pleasure.

When he stopped she groaned in disappointment.

'I know, honey,' he murmured. 'I know. But it's time to move on.'

She opened glazed eyes to watch him ease the vest back off her shoulders, letting it slide down her arms before lifting her stiff hands through each armhole. He tossed the garment aside then just stood there, his eyes glittering with a dark intent as they travelled slowly over her body.

The realisation that she was sitting on her dining table, naked to the waist, letting this man do as he pleased with her, should have filled her with shame. Instead, she was awash with a wave of wicked excitement. Her breasts were rising and falling, hot blood surging through her body with all the untamed power of a river in flood.

'So beautiful,' he said, stroking her hair back from her face then cupping her cheeks. His kiss was light this time, and exquisitely soft. His hands were equally soft as they stroked down her throat and over her shoulders. So when he suddenly took hold of those shoulders with a firmer grip and tipped her back onto the table she was startled into a muffled cry, her eyes widening.

'Trust me,' he said.

She wasn't semi-naked for long. Ten seconds later she was totally naked, her skirt and black satin panties having been peeled from her body in one expertly smooth movement.

The thought came to her that Nick had had plenty of practice at undressing women, and Linda was surprised at how jealous that made her feel. She frowned her bewilderment, but then he began smoothing his large, warm palms over her whole body, and she could think of nothing but the feel of his hands on her breasts, her stomach, her legs.

Soon she was consumed with the need to have him touch her even more intimately. She wanted his hands *between* her legs, wanted him to touch that spot which was more sensitive than any other part of her body.

But he had other plans for his hands, sliding them around and underneath her buttocks. When he lifted her slightly off the glass and his head began to bend, her eyes and lips rounded. She gaped down at the top of his dark head, flinching when his mouth closed over her navel, then freezing when his lips started travelling downwards. She could not believe he was going to do what it seemed he was going to do. Such an intimacy was outside her limited range of sexual experience.

There seemed to be no stopping him. And in all honesty she did not *want* to stop him. But old habits died hard, and for a while any pleasure was spoiled by feelings of embarrassment and vulnerability.

Gradually, however, the delights of his lips could not be denied and she found herself surrendering to the sweet pleasure of it all. Her mind swirled, her body squirmed, her heart pounded. She had never experienced anything like it.

She knew she was coming, and had no hope of stopping herself. The pleasure peaked, then broke in waves of electric ecstasy, her gasping cries echoing loudly in the room before eventually softening to the most sensual and satisfied sighs. At long last she lay quietly, her eyes closing as an ebb tide of the deepest peace washed through her.

Nick straightened to stare down at her. It had been difficult to distance himself from her passion. But he'd done it, and, amazingly, had found great satisfaction in doing it.

Such selflessness in lovemaking was a stranger to him these days. He only ever gave pleasure to gain it. Yet with Linda giving her pleasure had evoked a pleasure in its own right.

Nick's loins did ache for their own release, but he knew he would not take her right now as he would have any other woman he'd been with over the past few years. He wanted to wait till she was ready for him again, till she could join with him in further lovemaking to their mutual satisfaction.

A great feeling of tenderness swelled in his chest as he scooped her up into his arms and began carrying her from the room. That tenderness broke his stride momentarily.

'No,' he muttered, scowling denial of his feelings. But then her beautiful blue eyes opened to stare questioningly up at him, and he felt it again—that tenderness, that awful tugging at his heart which made him want to hold her close and love her as she had never been loved before.

Anger at such an uncharacteristic weakness steeled his legs and he forged on, flinging such stupid thoughts aside.

Concentrate on the sex, man, he lectured himself. That's all she wants from you. That's all any woman wants from you these days.

'Where are you taking me?' she asked.

'To bed,' he snapped.

'Oh,' she said in a disappointed-sounding voice.

Where in hell had she been expecting him to take her? Wasn't the dining table enough kinkiness for one night?

But then he realised she might have thought he meant to leave her there.

'Don't worry, honey,' he drawled. 'You won't be alone.'

CHAPTER NINE

LINDA woke to the sound of the shower running. For a few seconds she could not assemble her thoughts, but then her brain began to clear and she rolled over to glance at her bedside clock.

Five past midnight. She'd only been asleep a few minutes at most. It had been eleven-thirty when Nick had first carried her into this room.

Linda rolled back and sighed. She felt wonderful. Physically. But, at the same time, she was troubled. Why had it taken her thirty-one years to discover the pleasure and magic of making love properly? Why hadn't it been like this with Gordon?

But it hadn't. Sex with Gordon had been something she'd done more for him than for herself. Then later, when he hadn't wanted to make love much any more, she hadn't minded.

Hadn't *minded!* If Gordon had made love to her the way Nick had done she would have been devastated by his lack of desire for her.

Nick had shown her just now how it should be when a man and woman's body came together. There was no room for any shyness or shame or darkness. He'd shown her that downstairs, then when he'd brought her up here he'd continued in the same vein. First, he'd turned the lights on and left them on. Then, after laying her down on the bed, he'd undressed boldly before her, uncovering every inch of his male body without a single hesitation or qualm.

Of course it *was* a magnificent male body. Perfect in shape, and awesome in its power. He was all rippling muscle, his fitness evident in the superb structure of his chest muscles, not to mention the flatness of his washboard stomach. She'd been in a fever of anticipation by the time he'd finally stripped off his underpants, her insides twisting with a burning desire to be as one with this man. Amazing, really, when only a few minutes before she'd felt totally sated, her fires thoroughly quenched.

When he'd announced abruptly that he had to get some condoms from his rucksack in the family room Linda had coloured, for she hadn't even *thought* of protection. She'd still been blushing when he'd returned and joined her on the bed, then had been quite startled when he'd entered her straight away.

But he'd felt as fantastic as she'd known he would. It had been even better when he'd moved, his thrusts powerful and passionate. He'd lasted longer than she'd thought possible under the circumstances. And she'd done the impossible herself. Actually come, while he surged into her, without any manual help. She'd heard about vaginal orgasms but she'd never had one before.

It had been quite different from her earlier climax. Not so sharp, but infinitely more satisfying in both a physical and emotional way. She'd revelled in being able to hold him tight while her flesh contracted around his, had found intense pleasure in feeling his presence—not just inside her, but on top of her and all around her. She would never look upon the missionary position in a negative light again. It was incredible when it was right.

And it had been right tonight...with Nick.

Linda lay there, listening to the shower and worrying about whether she would ever experience such pleasure and satisfaction again. Nick's showering suggested that he had finished the lovemaking, that he would soon dress and leave.

She didn't want him to leave. She wanted him to come back to bed and sleep with her the whole night. She wanted to be able to touch him, arouse him, force him to make love to her again.

The shower snapped off and she groaned. Soon he would be gone, gone from her bed and from her life. Suddenly she felt not just dismay but also a quite overpowering desolation.

She smothered another groan when the bathroom door opened and Nick came into the room without a stitch on. But he didn't head for the chair which held his clothes, as she'd feared. He strode over to stand beside the bed, looking down at her with narrowed eyes while he roughly dried himself with a towel. When he tossed the towel aside, she was astonished to see that he was erect again.

'Glad to see you're awake,' he said. 'And that you've noticed my predicament. I contemplated a cold shower, but simply could not face it. Not when I knew my luscious Linda was out here, lying naked on her big, soft, sexy bed.'

He joined her on that bed, bending over to kiss her startled mouth. Her heart leapt along with her body.

'Do you think you might help a poor man out, luscious Linda?' he murmured thickly against her lips. 'Do I take your silence for agreement?'

He kissed her again, this time more hungrily, then reached over to the bedside table and extracted a new condom from the box. He pressed it into her hand, before lying back and sighing a deep sigh. 'You do the honours. My flesh is willing but my spirit is momentarily weak. Long, hot showers have a way of sapping my strength. Some of it, anyway,' he added with an ironic touch.

Linda elbowed herself up on her left side, staring down at the condom in her right hand then down at his beautiful body lying, outstretched, just waiting for her. She bit her bottom lip. How on earth could she manage to house him in this highly inadequate scrap of nothing that she was holding?

Suddenly, she was consumed by the most limiting and belittling feelings of inadequacy and awkwardness. Self-disgust quickly joined her dismay. Good God, she was an anachronism in this day and age! Thirty-one years old and as timid and inexperienced as a teenager.

'I don't know what to do,' she choked out with acute embarrassment. 'I mean...I've never...I mean I... I don't know how to do that.'

'Do what?'

'Put a condom on a man,' she confessed. 'As for making love to a man,' she added, trying not to go too red, 'I...I've never really done that either.'

There was no doubt that Nick looked stunned.

'Never?' he asked.

'No. Never.'

She wished she could have read the expressions

which flitted across his face. But they came and went so quickly. For her part, Linda felt awful. But what was the use of pretending to be what she could not be?

Nick's suddenly warm smile made her feel a bit better. 'Not to worry,' he said. 'A lot of women can't put a condom on a man. Not properly, anyway. Here, give it back to me and I'll try to manage when the time is right. Meanwhile, just put your head on my chest right here,' he directed, 'and snuggle up while I have a little rest. Then I'll see about us having seconds.'

'Seconds?'

'Well…seconds for me, honey. You're on thirds, you lucky devil.'

Linda wavered between cringing and giggling for a second, then just laughed and did as he said—put her head on his chest and snuggled up, her arms wrapping around his waist, her right leg lifting to lie along the top of his powerful thigh. It felt slightly uncomfortable, so she bent her leg to lift it higher and the side of her knee brushed the base of his penis.

'God, yes,' he groaned. 'Do that again.'

'What?'

'Your knee. Rub it up and down on me.'

She swallowed but did as she was bid, and he groaned again. 'Mmm, that feels so good. Now try it with your hand. Gently, now, but firmly. No, hold it right around. Oh, yes, that's it.' His groan sounded tortured. 'Don't stop. Just keep doing that.'

She had no intention of stopping. She was too turned on. A dark excitement was rushing along her veins and blotting out anything which even remotely smacked of guilt or shame or revulsion.

But soon doing it to him with her hand was just not good enough. She wanted to do for him what he had done for her, wanted to give him the ultimate thrill.

The thought excited her unbearably, and she released him to lever herself up and bend her head to his chest. Slowly her mouth began its erotic journey downwards, kissing and licking the skin as she went. His stomach fluttered wildly when her lips started travelling over it, the muscles stiffening once she passed his navel.

'You don't have to do that if you don't want to,' he said huskily. 'I really don't expect you to... Oh, God,' he moaned as her mouth made contact.

Using a knowledge born of memory of what had driven *her* wild, Linda spent a few tantalising minutes teasing and tasting him with her lips and tongue, working her way slowly down the full length of him. When at last she returned to take him between her lips, she felt his whole body tremble uncontrollably. When his hips began to squirm she drew him in even deeper.

'No, don't!' he choked out.

Linda was suddenly grabbed by her shoulders, her head wrenched upright and away from him.

'Why did you stop me?' she cried, her voice shaking. 'I wanted to do it. And you *wanted* me to. I *know* you did.' She was almost in tears, and her head was spinning.

He reached up and cupped her face, his fingers firm but shaking. 'Yes, of course I wanted you to,' he rasped, his chest still heaving. 'But I wasn't wearing protection and I thought... Hell, I wasn't expecting you to go all the way, and I was worried you might not really want to. I didn't mean to upset you. I was only thinking of you, Linda,' he finished with a ragged sigh, his hands falling away from her face as he slumped back on the pillow.

She blinked her astonishment. 'You were thinking of me,' she repeated, moved beyond belief by his sensitivity and selflessness. She could not imagine too many men stopping at that point.

But Nick had.

She leant over him to finger-comb his sweat-dampened hair back from his face, then bent to kiss him softly on the mouth. 'That's so sweet,' she murmured against his lips. 'But I would have gone to hell and back for you a moment ago; don't you know that?'

'Honey,' he said drily, 'you *took* me to hell and back.'

'Did I? Did I really?'

He shook his head at her, his smile rueful. 'Don't look so coy. You know damned well you did.'

'Was I good?'

'*Good?* You were damned good.'

His praise thrilled her to pieces.

'But when you were bad,' he went on drily, 'you were even better.'

She blushed furiously and he laughed. 'A little late for maidenly modesty, don't you think?'

'Yes, I suppose so.'

'In that case would you like to try putting the condom on yourself this time? It's a skill every sexually active female should master, you know. Safe sex is the order of the day, Linda, and not every man you go to bed with in the future is going to think to protect you.'

'But I—' She broke off, biting her tongue to stop the silly words from bursting from her mouth: *But I don't want to go to bed with any other man in the future. The only man I ever want to sleep with is you!*

Linda swallowed. 'Do...do you think I could just watch one more time?'

He sighed and reached for a new packet.

Watching him sent renewed darts of the most primitive desire stabbing through her. Understandable, perhaps, considering he was still stunningly erect. It would be difficult for any woman to look upon a man such as Nick, at the peak of his power and virility, and not feel nature's answering pull.

She found herself reaching out and following his expert fingers with her own slightly tentative ones, her stomach contracting violently at the feel of his flesh straining against its silken confinement. It quivered under her touch like some wild animal held captive against its will.

'Oh, no, you don't,' Nick growled. 'You've tormented me long enough.'

He rolled her over onto her back and entered her with a forceful thrust. Linda gasped, then moaned when his mouth crashed down upon hers. If anything, his primitive savagery evoked an answering savagery of her own. She lifted her legs to wrap them high around him, urging him into a deep and powerful rhythm, raking her nails down his back.

Her climax began to build immediately, taking her

breath away. She cried out at her moment of release, shattered by the intensity of her spasms. But then Nick climaxed as well, and, as she felt their bodies shuddering together, a well of emotion rose in her chest, bringing tears to her eyes.

When it was over and Nick went to roll from her she clung to him with all her might, keeping him imprisoned with her limbs and burying her face into his neck.

'No, don't leave me,' she choked out. 'Stay with me. Stay with me…'

He did, holding her till she sank slowly into the dark stream of sleep.

When she resurfaced several hours later, the other side of the double bed was empty and cold, and the house was eerily silent.

Panic-stricken, she called out his name. But there was no answer. She scrambled out of bed and ran, naked, through the house. She looked everywhere, even in the music room. There was no note. No Nick. Anywhere. His bike was gone. *He* was gone.

'No!' she cried, and ran through the house again, looking in the stupidest of places. Cupboards. The garage again. Out on the rain-soaked terrace.

She ran back inside, feeling sick and quite despairing. She tried to use logic and tell herself it was only to be expected. The man had warned her—he didn't fall in love. And he never stayed.

But nothing could stop the floods of tears. She hugged herself tightly when she started shaking uncontrollably. She didn't know if it was from the cold or the weeping. She just wanted him back, back in her life and in her bed.

'Oh, Nick,' she sobbed, and sank into a wretched huddle at the bottom of the stairs.

It was then that Rory woke and began to cry.

CHAPTER TEN

NICK rode into the convent grounds shortly before seven. He parked the Harley at the back of the U-shaped brick buildings, near the wing which used to be the noviciate but which now housed guests of the convent. The order hadn't had a new postulant in some years, their once strong numbers gradually being decimated by departures and death.

Nick could well understand why young girls these days didn't choose to become nuns. But it was a shame, in a way. It could be a good life for the right personality, although he had to concede that there had been some nuns in the old days who would have been better suited as wardens in a maximum-security prison.

Still, he was very fond of all the sisters still here. And more than fond of Sister Augustine. She was the closest thing to a mother he'd ever known, and, while he hated to admit it, Nick knew he would be very cut up when she finally passed away. The possibility of actually losing the person he cared about most in the world was something he hadn't really addressed before. Sister Augustine had always seemed invincible.

But she hadn't been well lately. It was one of the reasons he'd returned to Sydney—because one of the other sisters had got a message to him saying she thought Sister Augustine would benefit from seeing her favourite boy.

Nick moved across the gravel courtyard and up the steps onto the shaded cloister which ran around the courtyard. Everything was very quiet. At this early hour, the inmates would all still be in chapel, at six a.m. mass.

Nick hadn't been to mass in donkey's years, and he didn't aim to start this morning. He had an ongoing argument with God and was not yet in the mood to make up. He stopped in front of the door at the far end of the corridor, swung his rucksack from his shoulder and drew out his keys. For a few moments he fingered the little lantern which he'd lent Linda last night.

You've done the right thing, he told himself firmly. The only thing.

He grimaced as he thought of how she'd clung to him after that last time, how she'd begged him to stay. Nick suspected that if he'd still been there when she'd woken this morning she'd have tried every female trick in the book to make him stay longer—and one night would have become two, then probably three. Hell, he'd *wanted* to stay himself. So much that it had been bloody frightening!

He'd felt rotten, slipping out without a word. But staying would have been worse. It would have given her false hopes where he was concerned. As it was things had already been in danger of getting out of hand.

He'd known right from the start that Linda was in a vulnerable state, that she might start becoming emotionally involved with him if he slept with her. Nice women were like that. But, damn it all, he just hadn't been able to resist her.

With a bit of luck, when she woke, she'd hate his guts for being so cowardly—for seemingly using her like that and then decamping without even having the decency to face her the morning after, or the manners to say a proper goodbye.

Now she could get on with her life, find herself some decent, steady man who would provide her with everything she needed, not just sex. She was a beautiful woman. Beautiful and clever and sexy. Some lucky fellow should be only too glad to marry her, and be a stepfather to Rory.

Nick frowned at this last thought, then scowled. He jammed his key into the lock and twisted it.

Like who? he asked himself savagely as he pushed open the door and strode into the simply furnished cell. Most of the bastards out there these days didn't marry women who'd already had another man's kid. They screwed them silly, took them for all they were worth, then eventually dumped them for fresher, less complicated fields. If they ever did marry them, it was only to get their greedy hands on their money. Such men never cared about the child. They usually ignored them, or downright neglected them!

Nick kicked the door shut and tossed his rucksack in the corner before sinking down on the end of the narrow bed. The thought of anyone treating either Linda or Rory badly filled him with horror. Groaning, he propped his elbows on his knees and buried his face in his hands.

His head had begun to pound. He could hardly think straight. There he'd been, thinking he was doing the right thing in leaving—the *noble* thing. Hell, he'd been chock-full of nobility since he'd met the darned woman.

Yet, in reality, he'd only made things worse for her. Set her on the path to destruction. Given her a taste for what could ultimately be her biggest downfall. If she thought life had been rotten for her when the love of her life had died, let her see what life was like if she took a new lover who lived by today's selfish, amoral standards!

But it was Rory's fate which twisted Nick's guts the most. The poor kid didn't have a chance with no father, a mother who was having difficulty coping and an uncle who was bloody useless.

A sudden thought came to him and Nick's head snapped up. Damn it all, where were Rory's grandparents? Not Linda's parents; he knew they were dead. But what of dear old Gordon's parents? Surely one, or even both of them, had to be alive? Didn't they care about their grandson? Why weren't they giving Linda support? Why did she have to cope all alone all the time?

Questions whirled in Nick's head. Angry questions. He stood up and began pacing the room, muttering his frustration. He was still pacing when the door was suddenly flung open and Sister Augustine stood there, beaming at the sight of him.

'Nick!' she exclaimed happily, before hurrying into the room and hugging him. 'I thought I heard that noisy bike of yours when we were at mass. I came straight down here as soon as I could.'

She drew back and held him at arm's length. 'So what happened yesterday? When you rang you only said you'd been delayed on the road. I was a bit wor-

ried when you didn't make it home last night. Are
you all right?' She suddenly seemed to sense his inner
agitation, and scanned his face searchingly. 'Nick?
What's wrong?'

Nick sighed. He could never keep anything much
from Sister Augustine. She seemed to have a secret
antenna where he was concerned.

'I'm a little tired, that's all. I didn't have much
sleep last night.' And wasn't *that* the truth!

He turned away from those knowing grey eyes and
walked over to pick up his rucksack. Anything so that
she could not peer into his face and see his guilt.

'Something must be really worrying you to stop
you sleeping,' she remarked thoughtfully. 'As a lad
you were a hyperactive little devil during the day. But
once your head hit that pillow after dinner you were
out like a light and didn't wake till morning.'

Her words stirred something at the back of Nick's
mind and he frowned.

'For once in your life, Nick,' Sister Augustine said,
exasperation in her voice, '*tell* me what's bothering
you.'

'What?' Nick looked up, and the niggling thought
was lost. He laughed drily. 'Oh, no, you don't, Gussie.
You're my favourite girl and I love you dearly, but
I'm not going to let you browbeat me into confessing
all. If I want to do that I'll go see a priest.'

'Well, you and I both know you won't do that!
Still, the word "confessing" does suggest you feel
guilty about something. Maybe it would do you good
to get it off your conscience. And who knows? Maybe
I can help with some sound advice. I might only be

a silly old nun, but I've seen a lot of life in nearly eighty years.'

Nick shook his head and rolled his eyes. 'What am I going to do with you? I come here just to visit and see how your health is, and already I'm getting the third degree.'

'What do you mean, see how my health is? I'm perfectly fine.'

'No, you're not. You had pneumonia this past winter, and you didn't even write and let me know.'

'So how *do* you know?' she asked indignantly.

He gave her a wry grin. 'I have my methods.'

'I'll be having a word with Sister Agnes, I think,' she muttered, her lips pursing in irritation.

Nick placed his hands on her shoulders and peered down into her face. Her eyes were bright—probably from anger—but other than that she looked pale and tired. And she was shrinking, hardly coming up to his shoulders. Yet she'd been such a tall, strong woman. There was no use kidding himself—Sister Augustine was finally getting old.

'Promise me you'll start looking after yourself,' he said softly. 'I don't want to lose you, you know.'

'But you will one day, Nick,' she told him matter-of-factly. 'Death is a guarantee. And when you're nearing eighty it's just around the corner.'

'Don't say that!' His hands dropped away from her shoulders and he spun round to stalk over to the one window which graced the plain white walls. But there was no peace in staring out at the garden, *or* from Sister Augustine.

'I must!' she persisted. 'I must make you see!'

'See what?' He whirled to face her, his heart thudding.

'That the time has come for you to stop running away from life.'

Nick tried not to become angry with her. He knew she had his best interests at heart. But she just didn't understand. No one did.

'I am not running away from life,' he argued. 'I live life fuller than most people.'

'How? By never staying anywhere long enough to put down roots?' she scoffed. 'Or by sleeping with a different woman every other month? How proud you must be of that fact!'

He glowered a warning at her, but she ignored him by spinning away and walking over to shut the door. He heard her gather a deep breath before she turned to face him. She had that stern, no-nonsense expression which always preceded a lecture.

'Keep doing what you're doing, Nick, and one day you'll be a lonely, miserable old man with no one to care about you and no one for you to care about. I've tried to understand the way you've chosen to live your life these past ten years because I know how devastated you were by what happened to Sarah and Jenny. But Nick…do you honestly think Sarah would have wanted you not to ever love another woman? Or have another child?'

'Please stop,' Nick groaned.

'No, I'm not going to stop. Not this time. But the time has come for *you* to stop. Stop the running. Stop the grieving. Stop the guilt. It's become totally self-centred, and will ultimately turn self-destructive.

'Yet you're *not* a self-centred man. Not deep down

in your heart. You've got more capacity for love and caring in your little finger than most men have in their whole bodies. You're *made* to be a husband and father, Nick. And you're made to be one of the world's great artists! Yet you spend your life like some heartless, homeless hobo. It's got to stop, I tell you, before it's too *late* for you to stop!'

Her outburst finished, all the frustration and anger seemed to just drain out of her. Her frail shoulders sagged and she looked at him with such sad, sympathetic eyes. 'I'm sorry for speaking so bluntly, Nick. But someone had to say something. Who else is there but me?'

Nick was moved by her caring. But her almost brutal words had struck deep. Was she right? Had he become nothing but a selfish, self-centred bastard?

What bothered him most, however, was what she'd said about Sarah. He had never really thought about what Sarah would have expected of him.

But, now that he did, he suspected Sister Augustine was right. If Sarah had been standing here right at this moment she would surely have looked at him with disappointment and reproach in her eyes. She'd always been proud of him. How could she have been proud of the man he was today? He was not being true to himself. He was living a lie—not just because he'd abandoned his God-given talents, but also because of the lifestyle he'd adopted.

The boy who'd grown up without parents or siblings of his own had always wanted a family more than anything else. This deep-seated need had seen him marry young. He'd only been twenty when he and Sarah had walked down the aisle, with Sarah already pregnant. They'd been thinking of a second child before the accident had happened.

When fate had taken his entire family from him, Nick had turned his back on everything he'd once held dear and which had made life worth living.

His stomach began to churn with self-disgust. What he'd thought of as an understandable reaction, even a testimony to the love he'd held for Sarah and Jenny, had eventually become cowardice. He'd been afraid to love again, afraid to take another risk of being hurt like that a second time.

To what end? he asked himself now. Did he really want to become a miserable, lonely old man? Yesterday had shown him that, underneath, he *did* still want what he'd once wanted. He'd felt the pull in his heart when he'd held Rory in his arms. He'd felt more of the same when he'd made love to Linda.

As much as he'd tried telling himself it was just lust, he'd known underneath that he was lying to himself. He'd experienced just lust, plenty of times. This had encompassed much more. A wish to give *her* pleasure more than to take his own. A tenderness mixed in with the passion. What he'd kept calling nobility had really been the beginnings of true caring.

He'd been falling in love with her all along.

But could he make her fall in love with him in return after what he'd done? Would she ever trust him again? Maybe he'd burnt his bridges behind him by leaving...

Nick was surprised at the panic he felt at this possibility. It just showed how emotionally involved he already was with the woman.

'Nick? Nick, what is it?'

Nick took Sister Augustine's shoulders again, his heart racing as he made the sort of decision he hadn't thought he'd ever make again. 'Only good things, Gussie,' he told her firmly. 'Only good things.'

'Good things?'

'Yes. And, speaking of good things, you wouldn't be able to rustle up some breakfast for me, would you? I have a busy day ahead of me and I'll need all the energy I can muster.'

'Nick, make sense, please.'

'I will, Gussie, I will. Over breakfast. Meanwhile, I have to shave and wash some clothes. Which reminds me, what did you do with all my old things? I know I used to own a suit or two.'

'Oh, dear! I bundled them up and gave them all to St. Vincent de Paul less than a month ago. You hadn't worn them for years, and I thought—'

'It's all right,' Nick broke in. 'They probably wouldn't have fitted anyway. I'm bigger than I used to be. I'll go buy myself some new clothes. I might buy myself a new car as well.'

'Nick, if you don't tell me what's going on right now, I can promise you there will be no breakfast for you.'

Nick grinned. 'Blackmail, Gussie?' he teased softly. 'Whatever is the world coming to?'

Sister Augustine just crossed her arms and tapped her foot. Nick came forward and kissed her on the cheek. 'I give in,' he said on straightening. 'I'll confess.'

'I hope you're not going to tell me anything I don't want to hear.'

He smiled. She was going to be surprised but, hopefully, pleased. 'The thing is, Gussie, I've met this woman. A very nice woman.'

Her eyes lit up. 'Oh, Nick!'

Yep. She was pleased.

'But that's not all,' he added.

'It's not?'

'She has a child. A little boy, not yet one year old. His father was killed in an accident.'

Sister Augustine's eyes widened. Nick could see the hope in her face, plus the surprise.

He tried to swallow the lump which had formed in his throat. 'I think…that I might make a good father to that little boy. And I *know* I could be a good husband to his mother. Her name is Linda, by the way. And her son is called Rory.'

Sister Augustine's eyes filled with tears. 'Oh, Nick…'

Nick felt tears pricking his own eyes. He cleared his throat again. 'I need your help, Gussie. I blotted my copybook with Linda this morning and I'll have to work hard to win her trust—not to mention her love.'

'Anything, Nick. Anything.'

'Just keep being here for me. Keep telling me as it is. And don't ever lose faith in me.'

Tears spilled from her eyes and ran down her wrinkled cheeks. 'But I never lost faith in you, my darling boy. Never.'

He gathered her into his arms and hugged her tight. 'I know,' he whispered. 'I know…'

CHAPTER ELEVEN

LINDA was finding the morning interminable, despite Rory being surprisingly good. He'd played with his blocks on the floor while she'd watched the Sunday shows on television, then had gone down for a mid-morning nap without so much as a whimper.

Linda showered and dressed at that point, dragging on old stonewashed jeans and a pale blue shirt which was loose and comfortable. Her hair was left down to dry naturally and make-up seemed superfluous, although the remnants of the previous evening's mascara gave her eyes dark shadows.

She looked tired.

But she wasn't. She'd slept very well—when she'd actually slept. She was, however, very down and seriously disillusioned.

She contemplated ringing Dave and begging him to come over so that she could pour out all her woes to someone. But her brother would hardly be sympathetic over her sleeping with a man like Nick on the first day they'd met. Dave already thought her crazy and impulsive for having had Rory—she didn't fancy him calling her stupid and gullible as well, even if all his observations would be correct.

Dave would also be furious with Nick. He might even go all big-brotherish and pick a physical fight the next time he saw him down at the pub.

Linda didn't want that. Firstly, because Dave would

probably get splattered all over the pavement. Secondly, because in all honesty she couldn't say that Nick hadn't warned her. He'd told her the score from the word go.

It was just that she was having trouble accepting the reality that Nick had actually lived right down to Dave's low expectations of his character where women were concerned.

Linda conceded that, sadly, she *was* very naive where men and sex were concerned. She'd been misled by all those years spent with Gordon. Sex had obviously been a low priority with him, but, at the same time, Gordon's permanent presence by her side had been cosseting, preventing her from being acquainted too closely with other men and their more carnal sides.

She hadn't realised how important sex was to some men, and what they were prepared to do in pursuit of it. It seemed they could adopt all sorts of roles to get a woman into bed. They would do and say whatever it took, depending on the woman in question.

She'd been completely taken in by Nick, and had thought him something very special.

But what was the cold, hard truth behind his seemingly generous behaviour? Had he offered to mow her lawns hoping to meet her? Had Madge's accident proved to be an expedient incident in his secret plan to seduce his drinking mate's silly sister—the one with the baby and no man?

In retrospect, his gentle care and sweetness towards Rory seemed suspect. Men didn't care for babies that much. Certainly not someone else's. And then there'd been his over-the-top consideration towards *her*—

helping her set the table, for pity's sake, and even arranging for the meal to be delivered.

Linda grimaced at how she'd swallowed his act hook, line and sinker!

Her lips curled with a bitter self-contempt. She hoped she'd been worth the price. Given the amount of food he'd procured—and the quality—she couldn't call herself cheap. How much was a hooker these days? Fifty dollars a go? A hundred? Six decent three-course Italian dinners would run to three hundred dollars at least! Good God, no wonder he'd stayed for seconds—just once would have been damned expensive!

But as soon as she'd fallen asleep that last time he'd been off, slinking from her bed and her house like the conniving, cold-hearted bastard he was!

Revitalised by some self-righteous anger, Linda swept downstairs and set about clearing the debris from the dining-room table. She had to grit her teeth to stop herself thinking about what had happened on that table the previous night.

She was stacking the dishwasher with stabbing movements when the front doorbell rang.

Linda scooped in a deep breath then let it out raggedly. She was not expecting any visitors. And she certainly wasn't in the mood for the religious door-knockers who seemed to be targeting her area lately. She believed religion was a private and personal belief—she did not want anyone forcing their ideas down her throat, or lecturing her on her own doorstep.

Marching from the kitchen, she crossed the hallway at some speed, steeling herself as she yanked the door open.

'Nick!' she exclaimed, her heart jumping with instinctive joy before her brain kicked in and wiped the silly pleasure from her face. She tried to keep her eyes cool as they swept over him, but, damn it, he looked good. He was fresh and clean and sexy in blue jeans and a white T-shirt. His jaw was clean-shaven and his hair was neatly brushed back, giving her a glimpse of how devastatingly handsome he would be with a more groomed appearance.

'What are you doing back here?' she asked him in a cold voice. 'I would have thought you'd be halfway to Brisbane by now, or wherever you're off to next!'

His soft smile threw her. 'Now, Linda, don't be angry with me,' he said. 'I thought I was doing the right thing by leaving like I did.'

'I'm sure you did,' she snapped. 'Men like you are best soon forgotten.'

'You really are *very* angry with me, aren't you?' he remarked, that small smile still on his lips.

'And that's something to smile about, is it?'

'In a way.'

'What way?'

'It shows you care.'

'I do *not* care! I don't give a fig for you. You're nothing but a...a...a...'

'Bloody fool,' he finished for her. 'Yes, I agree with you. I should have stayed. I apologise. Will you forgive me?'

Linda felt her heart catch, despite common sense telling her to be careful. 'I—I don't know. I shouldn't...'

'Yes, you should.'

Linda was taken aback by his sureness. '*Why*

should I?' she demanded to know, crossing her arms and glaring at him.

'Because I have a proposition to make that I believe is in your best interests.'

'What proposition?' Linda asked warily.

'You need a nanny for Rory. I'd like to apply for the job.'

Linda gaped at him.

'Yes, I appreciate your surprise. I'm sure you weren't thinking of a male nanny. But there's no reason why a man couldn't do the job as well as a woman. From what I've seen of you, you're not a sexist or a traditionalist. After all, you had a long-term live-in relationship with a man which didn't involve marriage, or even your doing the cooking.

'Might I remind you that I am an excellent cook as well as an experienced baby-minder? Actually, this would not be the first time I've filled such a position. You could do worse than to hire me, I assure you.'

Linda didn't know what to say. She would not have been human if she weren't tempted. It would be every woman's fantasy come true to have a man like Nick to come home to every night.

But only the very naive would simply accept his proposition at face value. Linda's newly discovered cynicism about men and their motives warned her that this was not what it seemed.

'It would be very silly of me indeed,' she told him coolly, 'to hire a man I know so little about. I don't even know your last name! And I have only your word for it that you've minded children before. I would also expect proper references before I let anyone in my home on a live-in basis.'

'Ah, yes—well, I did think of that,' he said, and extracted a folded piece of paper from his back pocket. 'Here. Read this.'

She did. And her astonishment grew with each word.

> To whom it may concern,
> Nick Joseph has been known to me for his entire life, and I have no hesitation in recommending him for whatever position he may apply for. He is a hardworking and trustworthy man, with good Christian values. His generosity of spirit and sincerity of soul are valued by all who know him well. Children especially respond to him and he has in the past been responsible for at least one child's day-to-day welfare that I know of.

It was signed by a Sister Augustine of the Little Sisters of Saint Joseph, Strathfield, with a phone number attached.

Linda glanced up with startled eyes. 'A nun, Nick? I'm impressed.'

'I hoped you would be. Please feel free to ring Sister Augustine if you have any doubts.'

Linda was not about to be taken in that easily. 'And how is it that you know this nun?' she asked, suspicion in her voice. She hadn't forgotten all her recent doubts where Nick was concerned.

'She raised me.'

'She raised you,' Linda repeated blankly.

'Yes. I was left on the convent doorstep when I was a baby. The good sisters took me in, but it was Sister Augustine who was my main mother figure.

She's one of the reasons why I want a job in Sydney for a while. She's rather old, you see, and hasn't been well lately. I want to be close, in case she needs me or takes a turn for the worse.'

Linda was both taken aback and touched. So that was why Nick was a bit of a wanderer. He was an orphan with no real family except for this Sister Augustine. It was incredibly sweet that he was so attached to her that he was prepared to change his lifestyle to be of some support to her in her old age.

'Look, do you think I might come inside?' he asked. 'It's rather warm standing out here in the sun.'

Linda hesitated, and Nick waited patiently. .

'If I let you in,' she said carefully, 'I don't want you to jump to any conclusions. And I don't want you to touch me,' she added, bitterly aware of her weaknesses where this man was concerned.

'No touching,' Nick said, and held up his hands, palms out. But there was a definite gleam in those sexy black eyes of his which belied his supposedly innocent gesture.

Linda sighed. 'Come in, then,' she said. 'I'll make us both some coffee.'

'Over which I'll convince you of my good intentions.'

She slanted him a rueful look as he walked past her into the hallway. 'Let's not stretch credibility too far, Nick. You and I both know you have very few good intentions when it comes to the ladies.'

He actually winced at this remark. 'I see I have some way to go to redeem myself in your eyes,' he muttered.

Linda shut the front door, then turned to face him.

'Why should you care if you redeem yourself in my eyes or not? Or is it that you've returned not so much for a job minding Rory but to worm your way back into my bed?'

Nick eyed her thoughtfully. 'I could lie, I suppose, and say I don't want to make love to you some more. Or I could tell you the whole truth and nothing but the truth so help me, God, but I have a feeling you wouldn't believe that either. So for now I'll just say that, no, I haven't come back just to get you into bed. I really *do* want that job minding Rory. But, yes, if sharing your bed each night is a fringe benefit then I won't knock it back.'

Linda's head whirled at the thought of having Nick in her bed every night. She sucked in a breath, then let out a long, quivery sigh. 'Well, that's being honest, at least.'

He smiled a wickedly engaging smile. 'I *am* honest. Didn't you read that reference?'

Linda gave a short, caustic laugh. 'Mind if I test that honesty a second time?'

'Go ahead.'

'Did you really get that Italian food for free last night, or did you pay?'

He seemed to be genuinely astonished. 'What a strange question! Of course I got it for free. Why would I lie about something like that?'

'It crossed my mind this morning that it might have been part of a plan.'

'Plan? What plan?'

'Seducing Dave's silly, sex-starved sister.'

He just stared at her, then slowly shook his head. When he set determined eyes upon her and began closing the distance between them Linda fell back against the wall.

'You promised me you wouldn't touch me,' she protested in a breathless whisper when his hands closed firmly over her shoulders.

'This isn't touching,' he growled. 'It's making you see sense. Now, let's get this straight—I never had a plan where you were concerned. What happened yesterday just happened. Do I make myself clear?'

'Yes,' she agreed weakly.

'Now, let's not play games with each other, Linda. I'm too old for games. Are you going to hire me as Rory's nanny or not? I'll do the job in exchange for bed and board. Where that bed is located is entirely up to you. You're in control here.'

In control? She almost laughed. She was not even remotely in control, especially not with him being so close to her, with his hands upon her. She'd made him promise not to touch her because she'd suspected this might happen.

Still, she had to admit that Nick was quite convincing in his protestation of innocence. It seemed he hadn't planned to seduce her...yesterday.

But today was another story.

'Linda? Make up your mind, please.'

What to do? Send him away? Or surrender to what she really wanted to do?

'I...I...I'd like to give it a trial,' she choked out.

'A trial,' he repeated slowly, his eyes never leaving hers.

'Well...it might not work out,' she said defensively.

'No,' he agreed. 'It might not. But I think it will,'

he continued confidently. 'Look, I'll just go put my bike in the garage and bring my bag inside.'

'You…you want to move in right *now?*'

'Yes, why not? Don't you want me to?'

What she wanted wasn't the point! She might be a melting mess inside, but she had to *seem* to be in control. She was the employer, after all. Nick was the employee.

'Well, I suppose you can. The guest room is made up.'

'The guest room?'

Her chin lifted. 'That's correct. Take it or leave it.'

'I'll take it.'

'And you'll have a proper salary—none of this "just for bed and board" nonsense. I'll find out tomorrow what an average nanny earns.'

Nick smiled his satisfaction with the proceedings. 'Whatever you say, boss.'

Linda determinedly ignored the underlying excitement racing through her veins. 'If you cook the evening meals, I'll throw in the bed and board for nothing.'

'Sounds like a bargain.'

'We'll try a week to begin with,' she said in a vain pretence at practicality and common sense.

Nick frowned. 'That's not very long.'

'Long enough,' she said brusquely. 'Now, since you're moving in today you might as well come food shopping with me this afternoon.'

'But what about Madge?'

'What about her?'

'Wouldn't you like to visit her in hospital?'

Linda sighed a weary sigh. 'Well, yes, I would, but I get nervous taking Rory out in the car by myself.'

'But you won't be by yourself,' Nick said brightly. 'I'll go with you. After all, a good nanny goes wherever his charge goes.'

Linda looked up at him. How wonderful to have someone to help her with Rory! 'I really like the sound of that,' she said truthfully. 'But you don't have to if you don't want to. Even a nanny has Sunday off.'

'But I haven't got anything better to do for the rest of the day. Besides, I'd really like to see Madge. I rather took to the old girl straight away.'

'And she took to you,' Linda countered.

As did Rory and yours truly, she reminded herself ruefully. The man was a charmer all right.

And it seemed he wasn't the total bad boy she'd painted him in her mind. There was an earnest sincerity about him this morning which could not be denied. Plus an engaging honesty. She had to believe his story about Sister Augustine. It was just too fanciful to be a lie.

And he hadn't lied about wanting to sleep with her some more. If he'd claimed innocence in that matter she simply would not have believed him.

A thought crossed her mind and she laughed.

'What's so funny?' Nick asked.

'I was just thinking what would happen if Dave showed up here today and found you installed as Rory's nanny.'

'Mmm. What's the chance of that happening?'

'Little to none. But the idea of his shocked face rather amused me.'

Linda could see that the idea of Dave's shocked face didn't amuse Nick at all. She reached out and gently touched his arm in a reassuring gesture.

'Don't worry. Dave doesn't run my life. I will do as I please. And it pleases me to have you as Rory's nanny.'

He glanced down at her fingertips, then up into her eyes. 'You're touching me,' he said quietly.

'Sorry,' she said, her hand slipping from his flesh.

'Don't be,' he murmured, his eyes never leaving hers. 'You can touch me as much as you like. Wherever you like. Whenever you like.'

'Don't say things like that!' she protested, thoroughly rattled by the passion in his gaze plus the intensity of her own instant desire to do just that.

'Why not? It's the truth. Last night was incredible. I'd be insane if I didn't want more. But I have no intention of forcing the issue,' he went on, suddenly sounding very matter-of-fact. 'I just wanted you to know my feelings on the matter. What happens between us on a personal level is entirely up to you. But be assured I won't be charging you with sexual harassment if you want to change the sleeping arrangements.'

She stared at him and tried to still her thudding heart. 'I...I wish you wouldn't keep making provocative statements like that.'

He shrugged. 'Sorry. I'm not trying to be provocative—merely truthful. But, if it bothers you, I'll drop the subject of sex. For now...

'Meanwhile, I could really do with something to eat. Sister Augustine is a sweet woman, but breakfast at the convent leaves a lot to be desired. Porridge.

Yuk! And the tea you would not believe. What I would not give for some simple Vegemite toast and some decent coffee!'

Linda laughed. 'Well, I can just about manage Vegemite toast and coffee—I hope. But I might need you as overseer. I've been known to burn toast and even ruin coffee, believe me.'

He fell into step beside her as they made their way to the kitchen. 'You know, someone should really teach you how to cook.'

'Oh?' She slanted him a smile which was decidedly flirtatious. 'Are you offering?'

'I have been known to teach ladies a thing or two occasionally,' he said with the most delightfully straight face.

Linda almost cracked up at that point. 'Now that I *can* believe!'

He stuck his nose up in mock offence. 'Are you implying something of a decadent nature?'

Linda grinned. 'God forbid.'

'I'll have you know I was an altar boy! I even considered becoming a priest for a full twenty seconds one day while I was attending mass.'

'Oh? And what happened to sway your mind?'

'This girl came into chapel and knelt beside me. She was wearing a very thin floral dress and she had the biggest...um...' He made cups of his hands in his chest area.

'I get the picture,' Linda said drily. 'So what happened after church? Or shouldn't I ask?'

'Ask away.'

'Okay. What happened?'

'Not a solitary thing. She was a little old for me.

At least seventeen or eighteen. But I still got the message that celibacy and me were not on the same wavelength.'

'And how old were you at the time?'

'I can't quite remember. Probably around eight.'

'Eight,' she repeated, nodding. 'I can appreciate that. It was an eight-year-old boy who first showed me the difference between boys and girls.'

'No kidding. Do tell.'

Linda didn't even hesitate. Which was surprising. She was normally the reserved type when it came to talking about her personal life. But Nick was just so easy to talk to. She started by telling him all about that particular disaster, then moved on to the rest of her life over coffee and Vegemite toast. She told him all about her prudish mother, her rebellious but not very successful foray into sex at university and her passionate love of journalism and travel—which inevitably led to her life with Gordon.

'So you met him when you were only twenty-one?' Nick asked, munching into his third slice of toast.

They were both sitting up on the cane stools at the sleek white breakfast-bar in the kitchen.

'Yes. It was on my first trip overseas. I was in Paris, and staying in this hideously cheap hotel. I'd had my purse stolen during a trip up the Eiffel Tower, and was crying my eyes out on a bench in the park nearby when this handsome man handed me a handkerchief.'

'Wicked girl, allowing a perfect stranger to pick you up like that.'

'It wasn't like that! Gordon was a perfect gentleman.'

'Really? You mean he didn't sweep you off for an afternoon of lovemaking? In *Paris?*'

'Well…no…'

'*I* would have.'

Linda buried her instantly flaming face in her coffee-mug. 'I have no doubt you bedded half the female population of Paris while you were there,' she muttered.

'Not at all. You have me quite wrong, Linda. Just like your brother.'

'Oh, I don't think so. Not where women are concerned.'

Nick scowled, then sighed. Suddenly, he put down the remainder of his toast and slid off the stool. 'I'd better go and put my bike in the garage. Then you can show me to the guest room.' And he was off, striding out of the kitchen with a darkly disgruntled frown on his handsome face.

Linda stared after his decidedly angry body language. What had she said? Surely he could not be offended that she'd brought up his ladies' man status? He himself had admitted that he never fell in love, that he bedded women without any promise of future commitment, that always, in the end, he moved on.

Dismay at this last thought brought Linda up with a jolt. Surely she hadn't fallen in love with this man? Not in so short a time!

The idea was ludicrous. *She* was being ludicrous— and naive again. So he was charming and sexy. He was even sweet and considerate. She should never forget that he was also a self-confessed womaniser who never gave a woman what she cherished more than anything in the world: security.

Great sex was all very well. But, as Rory's mother, what she really needed was a man who would be there when the chips were down—a man who would look after her and her son, and love them both with a love that was steady and sure.

Nick was not that man. He was a ship that was going to pass in the night and she'd better not forget it. And if that fact was too much for her to bear, then she should change her mind right now and tell him to go.

Nick's return with his rucksack at that point put this last resolve to the test. Linda took one look at his handsome and now smiling face and knew she just couldn't send him away. She wanted him to stay.

She just wanted him.

CHAPTER TWELVE

NICK drove to the hospital, with Linda in the passenger seat and Rory strapped happily into his baby seat in the back.

Linda could hardly believe how good Rory had been since waking and finding Nick there. She was struck again by how competent Nick was with her son. He combined a relaxed manner with a much stricter firmness when required.

Rory seemed to respond very well to this kind of treatment. Suddenly, he knew who was boss of the situation and didn't try to take advantage, as he did when Linda was at sixes and sevens with what to do with him.

Linda could now see she'd contributed to Rory's habit of crying and grizzling during the day. Right from the word go she'd picked him up whenever he'd cried, even when there had been nothing wrong with him. Being a smart baby, he'd soon learned that crying brought swift attention from Mum. It had probably been a game with him. But it had worn her nerves to a frazzle, and had instilled bad habits in her baby.

'How come you *are* so experienced with babies, Nick?' she asked when they stopped at a red light. 'I mean, you have to admit you don't look the babysitting type.'

'Appearances can be deceiving,' came his casual

reply. 'I didn't always ride a motorbike or wander the world. The fact is I used to be a professional musician by night and babysitter by day.'

'A professional musician! On the piano?'

'Yes.'

'With a band?'

'No, an orchestra. But I did solo work as well, which paid a bit better, but not well enough.'

'Yes, I've heard it's very difficult for musicians to make a living.'

'It surely is.'

'So you babysat during the day to make ends meet?'

'Mmm. You could say that.'

'Girl or boy?'

'What?'

'Did you babysit a girl or a boy?'

'A girl. And speaking of babysitting, Linda,' he went on as he accelerated away from the lights, 'what's wrong with Gordon's parents? I mean, why is it that they haven't helped you look after Rory?'

'Oh.' Linda was momentarily taken aback by this abrupt change of subject, then troubled as to what she should say. To tell Nick that Gordon was not the father of her son would lead to a whole lot of awkward questions, all of which she didn't want to answer. Luckily, there was a way to satisfy Nick's very reasonable query which didn't require an outright lie, merely an evasion.

'They…um…they live in Hobart, Tasmania.'

'I see. Well, I suppose that *is* a bit far away. It's a pity they don't live in Sydney.'

'Mmm,' was Linda's noncommittal comment.

'Mmm,' came a little echo from the baby seat.

Linda's head whipped round to find Rory smiling his gummy smile at her. 'Mum,' she said to him. 'Mum. Mum. Mum.'

'Mum,' he repeated. 'Mum. Mum. Mum.'

Linda grabbed Nick's nearest arm and shook it violently. 'Did you hear that? Oh, my God, did you hear that? He's talking! Rory's talking. He said "Mum". His first word was "Mum"!' Tears of excited joy flooded her eyes.

'Linda, for pity's sake!' Nick protested. 'Are you trying to kill us all? Let my arm go!'

'Oh, sorry. I was just so excited.'

'So I can see.' Nick slanted her a wry smile. 'Does that make it all worthwhile, Mum, Mum, Mum?'

'Mum, Mum, Mum,' Rory immediately chimed in, and Linda's heart swelled with emotion.

'Oh, yes! Oh, you darling, clever little boy. Say it again. Mum, Mum, Mum.'

Rory obliged, then chortled delightedly as he bathed in his mother's beaming approval.

Linda had never felt so happy in all her life.

'Wait till I tell Madge!' she enthused.

'You won't have long to wait,' Nick returned. 'Here we are, with a parking space right outside the hospital. How lucky can you get?'

Linda stopped at Reception to check on Madge's room number, propping Rory up on the counter while the receptionist gave her detailed directions on how to find that particular ward. It seemed fairly complicated.

'Did you hear all that, Nick?' she said as she scooped up Rory and turned around, only to find that

Nick was nowhere in sight. Panic consumed her, followed by an overwhelmingly bereft feeling. Where on earth *was* he?

And then she saw him, striding towards her across the foyer from the direction of the gift shop. He was smiling, his arms full of flowers and fruit.

Linda felt his smile right down to her toes. It was a worrying response because she *did* know the score with this man, and falling in love with him was not part of the music.

His smile faded as he drew closer. 'If that scowl means you're going to make a fuss over how much this has all cost,' he said, on joining her, 'then don't. I can well afford a few mangy flowers and some measly pieces of fruit.'

'That is hardly a few mangy flowers,' she returned sharply, glaring at the huge arrangement of pink and white carnations. 'And you wouldn't have got that fruit basket for under twenty dollars, either. I insist on paying you back this time. And don't go telling me that the girl in the gift shop owed you one—that only works once with me!'

Nick's laugh was dry. 'All right, boss, I'll let you pay me back later.'

'In *money*,' she snapped.

Nick rounded his flashing black eyes in mock shock. 'But naturally! Why, Linda, whatever did you think I meant?'

'God only knows,' she muttered. 'Look, let's go find Madge's room before I totally forget the directions.'

It was a private room, fortunately, with no visitors present at that moment. Lunch had not long been served and Madge was just finishing her meal when they arrived.

Her face lit up with pleasure and surprise when she saw her visitors. 'Well, goodness gracious me, if it isn't Linda and Rory!' she exclaimed. 'And Nick as well! Are those lovely flowers for me? Oh, you shouldn't have. But I'm glad you did. Just put them here on this chest of drawers, Nick. And fruit as well. Oh, how sweet of you!'

'I did consider chocolates,' Nick said as he bent to kiss Madge on the cheek. 'But then I thought of your heart and decided fruit would be better for your health.'

'Oh, pooh! I'm already sick to death of hearing about my health. And I'm heartily sick of doctors. If they had my best interests at heart they'd let me out of here. I don't think I slept more than two hours at once last night, what with nurses popping in all the time, taking my blood pressure and heavens knows what. And, speaking of sleeping, was Rory a good boy last night? Here, let me give my precious darling a kiss and a hug.'

Linda brought Rory forward and Madge hugged and kissed him. 'Well, *was* he a good boy last night?' she repeated, with an expectant glance up at Linda.

'A perfect angel,' Linda admitted.

'Well, that's good to hear. Still, I certainly didn't expect to see you in here today, Linda. You must be tired after last night. And no way did I expect to see *you,* Nick.' Her eyes carried speculation as they went from Linda to Nick to Linda again.

Linda battled to keep the colour out of her face

while Nick, the cool devil, looked totally unconcerned.

'Nick offered to drive us in,' she said, by way of an excuse for his presence. 'And you've got no idea what happened on the way,' she raced on, clutching now at anything to distract her from her heating face. 'Rory said "Mum", didn't you, darling? Now say it for Madge like a good boy. Mum, Mum, Mum.'

Rory delivered like clockwork.

'But that's wonderful!' Madge praised. 'Not too many children start talking at his age. Oh, you *are* a smart little cookie, aren't you?' she told a beaming Rory, before glancing up at Linda again. 'So how did last night actually go? Pretty successfully, by the look of things,' she added with a wicked little twitch of her lips.

Linda's face felt really hot now. 'It went okay, I guess. I didn't have to cook. Nick had Italian food delivered from a friend's restaurant.'

'How enterprising of him. There again, I saw right from the word go that Nick was an enterprising kind of man. Responsible and reliable, too.'

Linda could not believe her ears. First, Sister Augustine had sung Nick's praises. And now Madge. What *was* it about the man that charmed the ladies so much? It couldn't just be his looks.

The acknowledgement that she might have totally misjudged Nick right from the start crossed Linda's mind. Admittedly, that bad-boy image mostly came from his riding a motorbike and wearing black leather. Linda appreciated now that Nick didn't really fit that image. Macho he might be, but he was not at all rough and tough. He was a gentle man, highly intelligent and widely travelled. And a pianist, no less!

'Yes, he certainly is.' Linda found herself agreeing with Madge, much to Nick's obvious surprise. 'That's why I've hired him as Rory's nanny.'

Madge gaped. 'Nick? Rory's *nanny?*'

Linda was startled to find herself reacting poorly to Madge's shock. Plus, perhaps, her unspoken disapproval. 'Yes, why not?' she challenged, a little sharply. 'Nick needed a job, and you saw for yourself how good he is with Rory. And he's minded children before, haven't you, Nick?'

'Indeed I have,' he said. 'Now don't you start worrying, Madge. I do realise this has all happened rather swiftly, but that's the way of things sometimes. I promise you that there is *nothing* for you to worry about. I'll look after your two precious charges with my life.'

Madge, who'd been frowning at Nick for most of this speech, suddenly smiled, at the same time exhaling a deeply satisfied sigh. 'Yes. Yes, I'm sure you will. Well, that *is* a load off my mind, I can tell you. The doctors here have forbidden me to do anything much for ages. In fact, when I leave hospital, I have to go and live with Jane for a little while. I was worrying about how Linda would cope with Rory. But now I can see everything's going to be fine,' she finished, with another happy-sounding sigh.

'You shouldn't have been worrying about me, Madge,' Linda said, frowning a little at the exchange between Madge and Nick. Some secret message had passed between their eyes which Linda couldn't quite fathom. Was Madge warning Nick to behave himself around her?

Probably, Linda thought ruefully. And Nick had faithfully promised Madge to do just that. In fact, he'd vowed to look after them with his life!

And, while that seemed to be going a bit far, Linda had to admit she'd liked hearing his rather passionate promise. One could almost believe he meant it. She also had to admit she liked having Nick around. He made her feel both cosseted and protected. She wouldn't have been a normal woman if she hadn't liked that feeling.

Madge's daughter arrived at that point, bustling in with a bouquet of roses and a big, hearty smile. Linda hadn't actually met Jane before, but she'd heard plenty about her. She was in her late thirties—a homely-looking woman and a very nice person, Linda quickly saw during their introductions. Just like her mother.

'So, we meet at last!' Jane said cheerily, holding the roses safely aside while she gave Linda a kiss on the cheek. 'And this is Rory.' She did the same for him and he beamed up at her. It seemed Rory was getting very partial to kisses on the cheek. Nick did it every time he picked him up.

'What a lovely-looking little boy!' Jane exclaimed. 'You didn't exaggerate, Mum. He's utterly gorgeous. Such eyes! And that smile! My, but you'll be a lady-killer when you grow up, won't you?' she said, chucking Rory under the chin.

Rory rewarded her with another of his widely engaging baby-smiles. Linda felt pride in her offspring, as only a mother could. Or a father, she supposed, her heart giving a twinge when she thought of Rory's un-known sire.

She no longer regretted having Rory, but she wished his conception had been different. She wished she had been madly in love with Rory's father, that he had been a true love-child—not the result of a de-cision made in her life when she'd been confused and unhappy and alone.

Still, you could not go back, could you? Like they said, there was no use crying over spilt milk.

'And you'd have to be Dave, I suppose?' Sue di-rected this towards Nick as she straightened. 'Now Mum didn't tell me how handsome *you* were.'

Linda and Madge laughed together.

Jane looked perplexed. 'What did I say that was so funny?'

'I'm not Dave,' Nick said. 'Though I am a good friend of his. My name is Nick.'

Jane looked even more perplexed. 'But I thought— I mean…'

Rory blotted his copybook at that stage by starting to grizzle.

'Here, give him to me,' Nick insisted, and took him from Linda's arms.

She didn't mind. Although not a fat baby, Rory was incredibly heavy to carry after a while. He was going to be a tall boy when he grew up, with strong bones and muscles.

Linda noticed that Jane was still frowning at Nick. 'Why did you think Nick was Dave?' she asked.

'Well, I just assumed. I mean, Rory looks rather like Nick—especially with those black eyes of his. I naturally thought they were related. From what

Mum's told me, I knew the only relative you had in Sydney was a brother named Dave so it seemed a logical guess.'

Linda nodded understandingly. 'I see. But no, Nick's no relative.'

'Nick was the one who rescued me yesterday, Jane,' Madge chimed in. 'And now he's going to rescue Linda.'

Linda blinked. 'Pardon?'

'I was referring to Nick's being Rory's nanny, dear.'

Jane looked taken aback at this news and Linda could appreciate her surprise. Nick was not normal nanny material, that was for sure.

'And being a good nanny whose number one priority is his charge,' Nick said from where he was holding an increasingly grizzly Rory, 'I think our little chap here is getting tired. Perhaps we'd better be going, Linda. Don't forget we still have some shopping to do on the way home.'

Linda suspected that Rory wasn't so much tired as bored. But she didn't say as much. It was a good excuse to bring the visit to an end and leave Madge alone with her daughter.

They made their goodbyes and headed down the corridor towards the lifts, past a couple of nurse stations. Linda noticed all the nurses turned to stare at Nick as he walked by carrying Rory. A couple of them whispered something to each other, before giving Linda almost envious looks.

What were they thinking? she wondered. That he was her handsome hunk of a husband and Rory their beautiful little boy?

If only, she found herself wishing.

She was to think the same thing again when the three of them went food shopping, Rory perched up happily in the baby-seat section of the trolley, Nick doing the pushing, while Linda chose the items as directed by her forceful new nanny-cum-cook. Several older women shoppers made admiring comments about Rory as they passed by. The younger ones just stared, green-eyed, at Nick.

'All the women in the supermarket assumed you were my husband,' Linda remarked on the drive home.

'Not necessarily. More likely they thought I was your de facto husband, since you're not wearing a ring.'

Linda pulled a face. 'God, I hate that term—de facto.'

'Very well. Live-in lover, then.'

'Much better.'

He slanted a very sexy smile over at her. 'I fully agree.'

Linda quivered inside, but refused to let it show. 'Don't go getting cocky on me.'

'Mmm. Now that's a deliciously provocative expression,' he said, with an equally provocative glint in his eye.

Linda shook her head at him, smiling despite herself. 'You're a truly wicked man.'

For some reason this observation didn't find favour, for his face suddenly grew serious. 'I can assure you that I am not,' he said stiffly. 'I see I will have to somehow further redress your opinion of my character.'

'Don't be silly, Nick. I don't really think you're wicked. If I did, I would never let you look after my son. But you *are* naughty when it comes to the ladies, aren't you?'

'Naughty? Define naughty.'

'You see sex as a strictly physical act, to be indulged in for pleasure alone. You don't need to feel any emotional ties with your partners to enjoy sleeping with them. And you change those partners with regular monotony.'

'In that case you must be naughty as well,' he pointed out. 'Or are you saying you'd formed an emotional tie with me before last night?'

'Touché,' Linda murmured. She'd set herself up for that one. And he was so right—she could not claim to have had any great bonding with Nick *before* spending the night with him. But something had very definitely happened *during* that night. Then today she'd seen more sides to the man, and she liked them all.

In fact, she was well on the way to falling in love with him, which was the most stupid thing she had ever done. More stupid than having a child by artificial insemination from a perfect stranger!

'Don't be so hard on yourself, Linda,' Nick said into her unhappy silence. 'Women tell themselves that all the time—about needing to be madly in love to enjoy being made love to. It's simply not true. A woman can feel lust as much as a man. Maybe not as often or as indiscriminately. But the same primitive sexual hormones run through female veins as male ones.

'You're thirty-one years old. You're in your sexual

prime, and not to be condemned because occasionally you need a man. If that man happens to be me on this occasion, then I feel both privileged and flattered. You're a beautiful woman, and I like you enormously. Hopefully you like me in return, because if you went to bed with a man you *didn't* like, then I would have no respect for you at all.'

'But I *do* like you,' she insisted. 'I do…'

'Well, then. Stop giving yourself a hard time. Relax and enjoy our relationship for what it can give you.'

'Which is?'

'Friendship. Support. Fun.'

Linda sighed. 'Those three things have certainly been in short supply in my life this past two years, I can tell you.'

'So you should grab them with both hands. And I haven't even mentioned the great food you're going to get! You're on a lucky roll, honey. Don't start looking gift-horses in the mouth.'

Linda had to laugh. 'I think I've just heard the most devious seduction technique ever devised.'

'Then you'd be wrong,' he countered, straight-faced. 'If you want me in your bed tonight, then you're going to have to ask.'

Linda stiffened. She'd always been long on pride and short on eating humble pie. 'Don't hold your breath.'

He shrugged. 'It's up to you.'

And it seemed it really was. Even after Rory was safely asleep for the night Nick made no attempt to close the distance which had suddenly sprung up between them with his assertion. They ate their meal—

a stunningly tasty stir-fry—in a brittle silence, then washed up together in an equally taut atmosphere. Linda was about to break, and scream and shout or whatever, when the telephone rang.

Sighing irritably, she dried her hands, and was hurrying along the hallway towards the telephone when Nick grabbed her arm from behind, whirling her to a halt. 'If that's Dave,' he said, 'don't tell him I'm here.'

'Why not? He'll have to know sooner or later if you're going to stay on as Rory's nanny. Or do you expect me to hide your presence in my house like a guilty, shameful secret?'

'No. Not for ever. But I don't want you to tell Dave just yet. Please, Linda. Do this for me. I promise if things work out this week, and I stay on, I'll tell Dave myself next Saturday.'

'*If* you stay on? What does that mean? Oh, I see. Mr Fly-by-night is giving himself a convenient opt-out,' she scorned in a harshly contemptuous tone.

'You're the one who said I was on trial, remember? If you want me to stay, I'll stay.'

'You will?' Her heart leapt with a wild, almost uncontrollable joy. 'Well, that's...that's good. Very good. Thank you. Yes, I'd like you to stay. Now I'd better answer the phone before whoever it is has a hernia.'

Linda picked up the phone, her heart still racing. Nick was staying. The thought was as intoxicating as it was exciting.

'Hello,' she said rather vaguely.

'Linda? Is that you?'

Linda pulled herself together. 'Yes, Dave, it's me. What's up?'

'You sound a bit strange. Is there anything wrong?'

'No, no, nothing's wrong.'

'I tried to ring you earlier but there wasn't an answer. Where on earth were you?'

Linda shook her head at his accusing tone.

'I was out,' she said. 'Shopping,' she added when she saw Nick's eyes flash her a warning. She quickly saw that to tell Dave about Madge's accident would lead to far too many awkward questions. On top of that, her brother would only offer her unwanted advice. He might even offer to come over personally, God forbid!

'Oh,' Dave said. 'Look, I just wanted to make sure you got someone to mow your lawn yesterday. I felt bad afterwards for saying no, but I was absolutely stuffed, love.'

'No worries, Dave. Madge organised someone for me.'

'Ah. Good old Madge. Whatever would you do without her?'

I'd hire a six-foot-four hunk in her place, Linda thought wickedly as her eyes locked with Nick's.

'I've no idea,' she lied. 'Look, Dave, sorry to cut you short but I must go.'

'Rory playing up again?'

'Something like that.'

'He's really given you a lot of trouble, hasn't he, love? Still, he'll eventually grow out of this difficult stage. By the time he goes to school it will all be smooth sailing.'

'Thank you, Dave,' she said wryly. 'That's a real comfort to hear.'

'Off you go, then, love. Bye.'

'Bye.'

She hung up slowly, her eyes never leaving Nick's. Unlike her brother, this man was not full of empty words. He was right here, supporting her, helping her. No doubt one day he would leave. She wasn't naive enough to believe he was going to change his lifestyle for her. He was a rolling stone. When Sister Augustine passed away, he would move on. Still, Linda didn't want to look back and think she'd wasted a moment of their precious time together.

'Nick,' she said, swallowing.

'Yes?' His dark gaze narrowed warily.

'I want you,' she choked out. 'And I need you. Please...take me to bed.'

CHAPTER THIRTEEN

THAT week would remain forever in Linda's mind as the most amazing of her life. She discovered undreamt-of delights and surprises, all of them provided by Nick.

On Monday night she came home to the sounds of an operatic tenor in full voice belting out an aria she recognised but could not identify. Had Nick found Gordon's Pavarotti CD collection? she puzzled as she hurried up the stairs.

But no, it was Nick himself singing in the bath, with an ecstatic Rory down the other end, splashing his arms around with all the flamboyant splendour of a miniature Italian conductor.

Linda was so astonished by the rich beauty of Nick's singing, she didn't notice his nudity for a full twenty seconds. But, once she did, their eyes locked and his voice suddenly died. They just managed to control themselves till Rory went to bed, after which Nick showed her more of his repertoire of creative talents, complete with encores.

The next night when she came home Nick was at the piano, playing a stirring Sousa march to an exuberant Rory who was perched up on top of the baby grand, clapping and kicking his little feet in time to the music. Linda was even more astounded by Nick's brilliant piano-playing than she had been by his singing. He'd admitted to being a musician, but clearly he wasn't any old musician—the man was a musical genius!

He confessed to her later in bed that he also played the violin quite well. Sister Augustine had apparently been driven to desperate measures by his hyperactive nature, filling all his leisure hours with lessons of one kind or another. Music and sport had been his main loves as a teenager. He'd played soccer and dabbled in gymnastics and the martial arts, these latter activities explaining his impressive musculature. He still did a hundred push-ups every morning and worked out with weights whenever he had the chance to visit a gym.

Linda told him that no way was she going to let him within sight of a gym while he worked for her. Sydney gyms were notorious pick-up joints, full of far too many attractive and very fit women prancing around and popping their pecs at men like him. He laughed and promised faithfully that his workouts would stay private, and strictly with her.

Wednesday, she had to work late—her main feature story for that month had to be changed at the last minute, due to a new royal drama. The magazine Linda worked for might be called *Aussie Woman,* but in the main it was filled with articles on international celebrities, of which Princess Diana was the mainstay. In truth, Linda was a bit disillusioned by the type of story she was required to write for *Aussie Woman.* But it had been the only decent-paying journalistic job she'd been able to get at the time. Now, of course, she needed to keep working to pay Nick's salary.

But he was well worth every cent, she decided when her son's very sexy nanny greeted her at the door that night, wearing nothing but jeans slung low on his hips. Admittedly, it *was* an exceptionally warm evening, but a semi-naked Nick was still a sight to tempt even the most jaded features editor.

'What's this for?' she murmured when he pressed a chilled glass of white wine into her hand.

He kissed her on the cheek and shut the front door before answering. 'I came across the two bottles of Italian wine that Gino sent over with the food last Saturday night. At the time, I thought it too powerful a drop for your sedate dinner party so I hid them in a cupboard. But it's just the thing after a hard day at the office.'

'He sent wine too? Whatever did you do for this Gino that he would be so generous in return?'

'I gave him some money when he needed it most.'

'And I presume you've never asked for it back?'

Nick shrugged his broad and distractingly bare shoulders. 'I had no need of it.'

Linda was impressed by his generosity and total lack of greed. 'Sister Augustine was right—you are a good man at heart. But, unfortunately, far too good-looking to inspire much goodness in others,' she added, smiling saucily up at him as she lifted the chilled glass to her lips. She drank gratefully, relishing its crisp dry flavour and its alcoholic kick.

'Ah.' She licked her lips, aware that Nick's dark eyes were riveted to her mouth. 'That certainly does hit the spot.'

'Don't drink it too fast,' he warned. 'Believe me when I say a glass or two of this particular vino and you're anyone's.'

'But you're the only one here,' she murmured, and

trailed her left hand provocatively down the centre of Nick's bare chest, raking her fingers through the dark curls which arrowed down to his navel.

He smiled the wickedest smile. 'So I am. In that case, have another mouthful, me darlin'. It's been a long day at the office for me too, and I need some serious relaxing...'

Thursday was just as memorable, with Linda working long and hard all day before finally coming home to Nick's wonderfully spoiling presence. The full body massage he gave her that night was the most incredibly relaxing yet highly erotic experience of her life.

With the magazine having gone to press, Linda had been given Friday off. She offered Nick the day off as well, if he wanted to go and visit Sister Augustine, but he declined, saying he'd spoken to the good sister several times on the telephone that week and had lined up a visit to her on the weekend.

When Linda woke on the Friday morning to a breakfast tray and a smiling Nick she sighed her complete happiness. 'I must have died and gone to heaven,' she murmured.

'You deserve a little spoiling,' he told her. 'Now sit up and I'll put this across your lap.'

As Linda did as she was told, she glanced at the bedside clock and gasped. 'My God, Nick! It's nearly ten! You should have woken me. Oh, I feel so guilty leaving you to do everything with Rory. I know he can be a handful first thing in the morning.'

'He's been as good as gold. Besides, that's what you're paying me for, isn't it?'

'Perhaps, but not when I have the day off. I certainly don't expect you to wait on *me* hand and foot, either.'

'I *like* waiting on you hand and foot. It gives me pleasure.'

She shook her head at him as he arranged the tray across her lap. 'If I didn't know better, I'd think you were trying to make me fall in love with you.'

He gazed down at her, his black eyes totally unreadable. 'Now that's an interesting thought,' he murmured. 'And am I succeeding?'

Linda's heart caught, then turned over. He was succeeding very well indeed. But she refused to take too much notice of this dismaying realisation, lest it ruin the pleasure of the moment. 'Now that would be telling, wouldn't it?'

'But you're not.'

'Not what? Telling?' She laughed. 'Certainly not. You have a big enough ego as it is, I suspect. Where *is* Rory, by the way?'

'In his cot playing with his blocks. I'll bring him in here, if you like. Pop him into bed next to you.'

'I'd better eat up these delicious eggs first. Otherwise they'll probably end up decorating the sheets.'

'You could be right. That son of yours is one energetic laddie. He'll be walking soon, you know. He's already pulling himself up onto his feet anywhere and everywhere. God help us if he turns out to be a climber—then he won't even be safe in his cot.'

Linda stopped eating mid-mouthful. 'I've been meaning to buy him a proper playpen. Perhaps I should get one today.'

'Good idea. I've got some shopping I have to do as well.'

'Oh? What?'

'I need some new clothes for the coming summer. And a car as well. Can't go taking Rory out and about on my bike, can I?'

'But...but can you afford a car?'

'I have some savings,' he said rather cryptically.

Linda could not see his savings amounting to much if he'd been flitting around the world on a regular basis and had rarely been in permanent employment.

She sighed her dissatisfaction with his using up whatever he had on a car. 'I could take the ferry to work, I suppose. That way you could have *my* car during the day. I don't like to think I'm putting you to any extra expense.'

'For pity's sake, Linda, I can afford a mangy old car. The only reason I don't have one is because it's suited my roving lifestyle up to this point to ride a motorbike. Now that I'm back in Sydney, I'll be wanting to take Sister Augustine out occasionally as well, and I can't see an eighty-year-old nun riding pillion on a Harley, can you?'

But he didn't buy a mangy old car. He bought a snazzy silver Ford Fairlane Ghia. And it took him all of half an hour from the time he walked into the showroom before he was driving out in the car.

Linda was stunned. He must have paid cash for the transaction to have gone so swiftly and smoothly. Either that or he had a great credit-rating! Dazedly, she followed him home in her small white sedan, and Nick insisted on moving Rory's baby seat into the back of *his* car then leaving *her* inferior model in the garage while they took off for some more shopping.

By the time he steered Rory's pram into the most

MIRANDA LEE 169

expensive menswear store in the local shopping mall, Linda was bursting with curiosity. 'Have you won the lottery or something?'

'No.' Nick began casually flicking through a rack of extremely expensive shirts. 'I told you, I have some savings. I also came in for a rather large compensation payment some years back, so don't you worry your pretty head about what I spend, Linda. I've been very conservative with my money for the past ten years and I'm in the mood for a small splurge.'

'That wasn't a small splurge!' she exclaimed an hour later as he piled plastic bags galore into the boot of his car. 'That was a seriously large splurge!'

His smiling eyes met her shocked ones. 'You're right. It was.'

'You're mad.'

'Oh, no. I've never been saner.'

'All right, then *I'm* mad—because I don't understand what's going on here. Why do you need all those clothes? It's not as though you need clothes for work.'

His grin was very wicked as he bent to kiss her on the mouth. 'You're right there, honey. My boss prefers me to wear as few clothes as possible.'

'Nick, stop it!' Her face flamed and she felt like shaking him. 'I want some answers and I want them now!'

'Very well. I want you to be proud of me when we go out together to dinner, and the theatre, and the opera.'

'Dinner?' she repeated blankly. 'The theatre? The opera?'

'Definitely the opera. That's my favourite. I *adore* opera. You will go with me, won't you?'

'Well, of course I will. It's just that…that…'

'That what? Don't worry about Rory. Madge will come home eventually and she won't mind babysitting her precious darling on the odd Saturday night.'

Linda didn't know what to say. Common sense and a dash of cynicism told her she was living a fantasy here, that it could not last. But dear God, she prayed, please don't let it end just yet.

'Is there anything else wrong?' he asked, frowning down into her pained eyes.

'No,' she said weakly.

'Then let's go get Rory that playpen.'

They didn't just get him a playpen. Nick was stuck in the toy section for ages, buying Rory more toys in one hour than her son had been bought in his whole little life so far.

Actually, that wasn't hard. Rory did not have a lot of toys. He had no grandparents to spoil him; there was only herself and Madge. Dave was not a spoiling kind of uncle. He'd produced the mandatory teddy bear when Rory had been born, but not a thing since.

Most of the toys Nick bought were designed to amuse, stimulate and satisfy Rory's quick mind, with a couple of big, cuddly soft animals thrown in. And while she was touched there was one purchase which made Linda wince. It was a drum.

'Oh, no, Nick, not a drum!' she wailed.

His handsome face set into firm lines. 'Yes, a drum! Rory can learn to beat time when I play the piano.'

'But…but…'

'No buts! Rory has definite musical talent. I aim to foster that talent.'

Linda bristled for a moment. *She* was the mother here, wasn't she? *She* would decide what talents in Rory would be fostered, thank you very much! 'Do you, now?' she said waspishly.

'I do indeed. You hired me to be your son's nanny because he needed someone who would cater to his special needs. *I'm* that someone, so butt out on this, boss. I know best. I'll take the drum too,' Nick told the hovering salesman, who took the brightly coloured instrument and added it to the impressive pile of purchases.

Linda gave in gracefully, not least because Nick in a forceful mood made her go weak at the knees. But she still had to say something when she saw how much the bill came to. Hesitantly, she tapped Nick on the shoulder while they waited for the purchases to be put into bags.

'What?' Nick said sharply.

'I can't let you pay for all this.'

'You have no say in the matter. This is *my* treat.'

'But...but...'

'Linda, don't spoil my fun, please.'

'Your fun?'

'Yes.'

She was about to protest again when he gave her an exasperated glare. Linda fell resignedly silent. Nick, she realised, was one of those reckless spendthrifts whose money burnt a hole in their pockets. No doubt most of that compensation payment he'd mentioned was now well and truly gone.

'You are too generous for your own good,' she said

once they reached the privacy of the car park. 'You'll have no savings left soon if you keep giving money away and spending it on others.'

'But I *enjoy* giving money away,' he said simply. 'And spending it on others. What good is money if you don't enjoy it?'

She just shook her head at him, but she was smiling. Part of Nick's charm was his being different from most other men. He called himself cynical, but there had been a boyish exuberance about him today as he'd gone about buying those toys. His black eyes had glittered with a bright, innocent pleasure. Nick had a lot of sides to him, but this was the side she loved the most. He could be so sweet.

'I think we should be getting home before you decide to buy the whole shopping mall,' she advised, with a teasing warmth in her voice.

'Mmm. Now that's a thought. What do you think, Rory, m'lad?' He unbuckled Rory from his pram and hoisted him up high over his head. 'Shall I buy the shopping mall? No? Just the toy shop, eh? Good thinking, my boy. I like a lad who has his priorities right.'

Linda laughed while Rory chortled delightedly from his great height. Nick lowered him and gave his chubby cheek another of those kisses he bestowed without thinking. Linda's heart contracted, as it always did when he kissed Rory. Nick was a toucher, a tender and sensual man, always kissing and cuddling Rory, always kissing and cuddling *her*. She could not get enough of his kisses and cuddles, could not get enough of *him*.

'Come on, let's go,' she said, trying not to sound

too desperate to have him back home, alone with her. But she knew that after such an extended shopping expedition this afternoon Rory would be happy to go to bed even earlier than his usual seven o'clock. And he would sleep like a top!

She was right: by seven-thirty Rory was sound asleep. They'd eaten and cleared away, and the long evening alone together stretched deliciously ahead.

Linda normally waited for Nick to make the first move in the lovemaking department—and she rarely had to wait long. But this time she felt too impatient to wait even a minute or two.

So she snuggled up to him on the sofa in the family room, where he was sitting watching the television, and lifted her lips to be kissed. He did so ever so gently, one hand cupping her face as he sipped at her mouth, then touched her tongue-tip with his own. A wave of the sweetest pleasure rippled through her and she sighed.

'I love it when you sigh like that,' he whispered against her mouth.

'I love it when you make me sigh,' she murmured back.

He made her sigh several times before he stopped abruptly.

'Linda…'

She heard the wariness in his voice and snapped instantly out of her dreamy state, her chest squeezing tight.

'No.' She almost groaned. 'Don't say it.'

'Don't say what?'

'Whatever it is you don't really want to say.'

'But I *do* want to say it. It's just very difficult, that's all.'

Linda jerked upright out of his arms, swinging her feet back onto the floor, her shoulders hunched in defence of what was to come.

'What is it? Another warning about knowing the score? Or a reminder that you reserve the right to leave without giving notice? God, Nick, why were you so nice to me this last week if all you mean to do is leave in the end?' she said painfully. 'Why be so nice to Rory? Why make him adore you as he so obviously does? Why make *me* adore you?'

She glared her frustration over her shoulder at him, her mouth and eyes hard even while her heart was breaking. 'What a fool I was to believe all that rubbish you said in the toy shop today about fostering Rory's talents. You can't stay long enough anywhere to foster *anyone's* talents, not even your own. I tell you what— why don't you do Rory and me a real favour and just go right now?' she flung at him, leaping to her feet and marching across the room to stand at the windows.

She kept her back to him because tears had flooded her eyes and she was trying to hold herself together by hugging herself, her fingertips digging cruelly into her flesh.

But oh, dear God, the black despair in her heart! She hadn't appreciated till this moment just how deeply she'd fallen in love with Nick. She'd loved Gordon, but this was different. This was total. Nick had become as essential to her existence as the air she breathed. The thought of life without him was unbearable!

When his hands curled over her shoulders and he pulled her back against him she shuddered violently, wanting to wrench away but unable to.

'I don't want to leave,' he told her passionately, and her heart just stopped. 'I want to stay here with you and Rory for the rest of my life. But not as Rory's nanny—I want to be a real father to your son, Linda. And I want to be your husband, not your lover. I love you, Linda, with all my heart—that's what I was finding so difficult to say. I love you.'

The air around Linda suddenly felt thick and heavy. Her head spun with Nick's words. The room went out of focus and she turned slowly in his arms and lifted her blurred eyes to his. 'You love me?'

'More than I would ever have thought possible. And I love Rory too. I'll be a good father to him, Linda. I promise you that.'

Linda could not speak; she was too choked up. Nick loved her. And he loved Rory. He wanted to marry them.

'Oh,' was all she could manage, sliding her arms around Nick's waist and resting her head against the warm expanse of his chest. The tears spilled down her cheeks then, and she began to weep with happiness.

Nick's arms tightened around her. He had never felt anything like the feeling which whooshed through him now as he hugged Linda close, then stroked her head. He'd loved Sarah, but it had been a younger and more selfish love. His love for Linda was much more mature. He sought to give, rather than take. To truly cherish and protect.

A special bond had already sprung up between

them, he believed. And between Rory and himself. He felt so strongly about this woman and her son, it sometimes made him marvel. He had never believed he would ever love anyone ever again, not like this—so totally and without any fear or trepidation.

The only risk there'd been, once he'd accepted his unexpected feelings and decided to go after what he wanted, had been whether he could make Linda truly fall in love with him. He'd worried a little that her attraction to him might be strictly sexual.

But her earlier angry outburst, then her touching tears, told him everything he needed to know. She loved him. She, really truly loved him. God was indeed merciful.

'Don't cry, my darling,' he soothed. 'There's no reason to cry…'

She smiled up at him through her tears. 'I know.' She hiccuped. 'I'm just so…h-h-happy.'

He smiled back and wiped the tears from her cheeks with his fingertips. 'Do you always cry when you're this happy?'

'I don't know. I've never been this happy before,' she choked out. 'Or so in love before. Oh, Nick, are you sure? Are you absolutely sure? I mean…you said you never fell in love, and that you weren't a marrying man. And that…that you didn't want commitment.'

'Yes. And I meant it at the time. But that was before I fell in love with you. I still tried to run from that love, Linda. I'd be lying if I didn't tell you that when I left this house last Sunday I had no intention of returning. But a certain Sister Augustine made me see what a fool I was being, and once I saw the light

I vowed that nothing was going to stop me coming back and winning your love in return.'

'Oh, Nick...'

He swallowed, knowing that he had to tell her the whole truth. There could be no secrets between them, nothing held back. But, dear heaven, a huge lump was forming in his throat with just the thought of speaking about what he had refused to speak about for so long.

'There...there's something else I have to tell you,' he said, his voice strangled with emotion.

Linda's eyes carried a momentary cloud, but then they cleared. She reached up to cradle his face with gentle hands. 'You can tell me anything, Nick,' she said simply and with such a trusting love that he almost broke down right then and there.

He cleared his throat and moved back far enough so that her hands fell away from his face. He had to get a firm handle on the emotions welling up within him, and he could not do that with her touching him.

'I find it very hard to talk about this, Linda. You...you'll have to be patient with me.'

She nodded and said nothing. Merely waited. Patiently. Lovingly.

Nick took a deep breath and just started. 'After I finished school I went to the Sydney Conservatorium of Music. When I was nineteen, I met this girl, Sarah. She was a secretary there. She was twenty, a year older than me. A very pretty girl. Fair, with lovely green eyes.'

Nick swallowed a couple of times, but nothing helped the dryness in his mouth or the thickness in his throat. 'We fell in love, and within months Sarah was pregnant. We got married. Which wasn't a problem—I'd always planned to marry young and have the family I'd never had. Jenny was born six months after our wedding. She was…a beautiful little girl. A joy…'

Nick cleared his throat more noisily and struggled on. 'By then I was making a name for myself as a concert pianist. I'd won a couple of competitions and received some rave reviews. But, of course, none of that earns you much money, so after Jenny was born Sarah went back to work. I became a househusband during the day, minding Jenny so that I could practise. Then at night and at the weekends I would play the piano for extra money in restaurants and clubs. We didn't have much, but we were happy.'

A band began tightening around Nick's chest and he could hardly breathe. He began speaking in short bursts.

'A couple of days before Jenny's third birthday Sarah took a day off work…to take Jenny shopping… She wanted me to come too… It was raining, you see…Sarah didn't like driving in the rain… But there was this big competition coming up, with fifty-thousand dollars in prize money… I thought I could win… I saw that day as one of uninterrupted practice, with no Jenny to distract me…

'Sarah and I had a bit of a tiff before she left that morning…she said I was being selfish… I know she didn't really mean it, but afterwards…when they came and told me about the accident…and I had to go and identify their bodies…I…I…'

He stopped, scooped in a deep breath and prayed for composure. 'They said it wasn't her fault. There was this truck which ran through a red light…the driver was on drugs... When I found out it wasn't a genuine accident, I just went crazy... I took the trucking company to court, proved they knew their drivers were taking pills and got this big settlement...two million dollars... But no amount of money could bring them back, or make me feel less guilty...'

Suddenly, he could not go on. His eyes were awash and there was a vice around his heart. Linda came forward and took his arm, and sat him back down on the sofa. She sat down beside him and put her arm around his shoulders. He leant forward, his head sinking into his hands in a vain effort to hide his tears.

'It's all right, Nick,' she said softly. 'All right to get upset. All right to cry. I cried buckets for Gordon. Cry for your Sarah and Jenny, my darling. Cry...'

'Oh, God,' he groaned, and then simply could not stop the dam of emotion from breaking free. It spilled forth and he sobbed his heart out, clinging to Linda as he had never clung to anyone before. She cried too, cried with him and for him. And all the while she held him close, never letting him turn from her to hide his distress.

It was an incredibly emotional and bonding experience, a stripping away of everything but the most elemental. They clung and cried, till finally there were no tears left. And it was as they lay emotionally spent in each other's arms that they reached out for one another in the most basic way a man and woman could, kissing at first, then touching, then finally tearing at each other's clothes, their passion and need flaring with amazing speed and intensity.

Nick took her quickly, revelling in the feel of her

naked flesh around his, exultant when his seed spilled hot and unprotected into her waiting womb.

'Nick,' she cried out as she climaxed too, her body contracting fiercely around his. 'Oh, Nick...'

Exhausted, he groaned, then laid his sweating brow between her breasts. All he could think about was that maybe they might have just conceived a child. Yet he didn't mind; didn't feel afraid at all. In fact, the thought thrilled him to pieces. A little brother or sister for Rory—what a family they would be!

His arms slid around Linda and he held her to him, vowing never to let her go.

Unfortunately, five minutes later he had to.

Because the doorbell rang.

CHAPTER FOURTEEN

THEIR eyes met, wide, alarmed.

'Are you expecting anyone?' Nick asked, already off the sofa and pulling on his jeans.

'No.' Linda leant down and rescued her undies from the floor.

'Could it be Dave?'

'I doubt it. Not on a Friday night. He always works on a Friday night.'

'It might be Madge,' Nick ventured. 'She might have come home to pick up some things and decided to drop in.'

'Yes. Yes, that could be who it is.'

The doorbell rang again.

'Do you want me to go down and answer it while you get dressed?' Nick asked.

'If you would, please. Thanks.'

'No trouble.'

Dave was growing impatient by the time he rang the bell a second time. He knew Linda was home. All the lights were on. Why wasn't she coming to the door? What was she doing in there?

He jabbed the doorbell a third time. Now he could hear someone coming, and his heart began to thud with escalating nerves.

He still could not believe what he'd heard at the office today. But Mary was not one to lie. She was

181

positive she'd seen Linda with a tall, dark-haired, good-looking hunk today, shopping for toys of all things! He'd asked Mary to describe this hunk in more depth and, as improbable as it was, he'd sounded disturbingly like Nick.

Dave had found it impossible to concentrate after that. As soon as his column was presentable he'd handed it over and made his excuses.

'Family emergency,' he'd said.

And it certainly was, if somehow Nick had met Linda.

The door opened and Dave's worst nightmare materialised. For there stood Nick, wearing nothing but a pair of jeans. Then he saw Linda, hurrying down the stairs still doing the buttons up on her blouse. Any fool could have seen what had been happening between them.

'It *is* your brother,' Nick told her drily. 'Now, don't jump to conclusions, Dave,' he went on when he saw the look on Dave's face. 'This is not what it seems.'

'You womanising bastard!' Dave pushed Nick square in the chest, forcing him to stagger backwards.

'Dave, don't!' Linda cried, rushing over to wind both her arms around one of Nick's huge biceps in a protective gesture.

Dave could not believe the way she looked up at Nick. Love burned from her eyes, hot and obsessive.

Nick put one of his large hands over hers and patted it. 'Don't worry, Linda. Dave will calm down once he knows the truth.'

'What truth?' Good God, had he run into Linda and Rory at some time and somehow recognised his son?

'That I've fallen in love with your sister,' Nick

said. 'It was me who came to mow her lawn last Saturday. To cut a long story short, Madge had a bad turn and I stayed on to mind Rory till Linda came home. When we met, we were instantly attracted. Because I wanted to spend more time with Linda I offered to mind Rory for her while Madge was out of action, and I've been here ever since. Tonight I asked Linda to marry me, and she said yes. You *did* say yes, didn't you, darling?'

'Oh, yes.' She was fairly glowing as she looked up at Nick.

Dave was totally thrown. This was just so incredible! He could hardly take it all in.

'You said yes to marriage after only knowing Nick a week?' he asked dazedly.

'Yes,' she repeated firmly. 'I love him, Dave. He's a wonderful man. And he loves Rory too. Would you believe that? I thought I would never find a man who would love my son as much as I do.'

Dave looked from one to the other and realised they had no idea. 'You haven't told Nick, have you?' he said to Linda.

She looked a little guilty. 'No. Not yet.'

'Told me what?'

'Gordon is not Rory's father,' Dave said.

'Dave, for pity's sake,' Linda objected. 'Did you have to tell him so bluntly?'

'Not Gordon's?' Nick was frowning.

Linda grimaced. 'I...I meant to tell you, but it never seemed the right moment. And I didn't want you to think badly of me.'

'Who, then?' Nick asked, obviously bewildered.

Linda groaned. 'It sounds awful, but I don't rightly

know. I mean, before Gordon died he'd promised me
a baby, and then, afterwards, I thought…if I just had
a baby…I would have something to live for…'

Dave could see that the penny was beginning to
drop for Nick. He'd gone quite white, before giving
Dave a shocked look. An oblivious and embarrassed
Linda kept rattling on.

'I know it was silly of me, but I asked Dave if he
knew anyone who might be prepared to be an anony-
mous sperm donor—someone who had all the quali-
ties I wanted in the father of my baby. Someone good-
looking and clever and creative and—'

She broke off abruptly, paling herself as she looked
from a now smiling Dave up to a visibly moved Nick.
'You,' she rasped. 'It was *you*. You're Rory's father.'

'It seems so,' he said thickly. 'But I didn't know
the sperm was for you. Dave told me it was for a
married lady, and that it didn't take. I had no idea I
had a son.

'A son,' Nick repeated, his handsome face twisting
with the most heart-wrenching expression. 'Rory's my
son.'

'*Our* son,' Linda reminded him.

He stared down at her. 'Yes, *our* son,' he repeated,
then threw his arms around her and whirled her
around, shouting and laughing.

Dave could not help but be moved by their happiness. Who would have believed it all? Pity Nick
doesn't have any money, he thought. But there again,
you can't always have everything.

He closed the front door behind him and
said, 'Ahem.'

They broke apart and looked at him with a mixture of gratitude and exasperation.

'You lied to me,' Nick said, black eyes blazing with reproach. 'But I guess I'll have to forgive you, now that we're related. Still, I'd like to see some improvement in your uncling. It has left something to be desired, you know. A boy like Rory needs a lot of attention and guidance.'

Wow, Dave thought. He really does already love the boy. Such passion and intensity. For a second there, I thought he was going to thump me.

Dave decided a change of subject was called for. 'Er…when are you two getting married?'

'As soon as possible,' came Nick's firm reply.

'Would I be out of order if I asked how you intend to provide for my sister?'

'You would.'

'You can't live on love alone, you know.'

'Yes, we can,' Nick assured him. 'But if it's worrying you I have money, Dave. Plenty of it.'

'*Really?* How come?'

'It's a long story and not one I care to tell at this moment. Right now, Linda and I are going upstairs to look at our son together. You are welcome to join us, Uncle Dave.'

The three of them went upstairs, stood beside the cot and stared down at the sleeping infant.

'Madge's daughter was right,' Linda whispered. 'He *does* have your eyes, Nick. And your chin.'

Nick reached down and stroked a curl back from Rory's forehead. His heart was so full he could not speak at that moment.

Linda looked over at her brother. 'You chose well, Dave,' she said, smiling at him.

He smiled back. 'I thought so.'

'Has he been christened?' Nick asked, finding his voice at last.

'Not yet,' Linda said.

'I would like him christened soon, if that's all right by you, Linda.'

'Of course.' Anything Nick wanted was all right by her.

'And I'd like to take him to see Sister Augustine tomorrow. She's going to be so thrilled.'

'So will Madge when I tell her,' Linda said.

Both of them sighed and the child slept on, oblivious of the joy he had brought.

Nick looked lovingly down at his son and determined that first thing in the morning he was going to start teaching Rory how to say 'Dad'.

Linda smiled down at her son and thought how very likely it was that she had conceived a brother or a sister for Rory tonight—it was right in the middle of her cycle.

Dave just stood there and thanked the Lord that it had all turned out for the best. He was not a religious man, but that night his faith was renewed.

God did, indeed, work in mysterious ways.